SACRAMENTO PUBLIC LIBRARY
828 "I" Street
Sacramento, CA 95814
05/16

D0978364

MAN AND WIFE

MAN & WIFE

STORIES

\\\

BY KATIE CHASE

A
STRANGE
OBJECT
Austin, Texas

The stories in this collection have appeared in slightly different form in the following publications:

"Man and Wife," in the *Missouri Review,* "Bloodfeud," in *ZYZZYVA,* "Every Good Marriage Begins in Tears," in *Narrative,* "The Hut" on *Joyland* and *Byliner,* and "Pater Noster" in the *Literary Review.*

"Man and Wife" was also featured in the anthologies *Pushcart Prize XXXIII: Best of the Small Presses* (Pushcart Press, 2009) and *The Best American Short Stories* (Houghton Mifflin Harcourt, 2008).

Published by
A Strange Object
astrangeobject.com

© 2016 Katie Chase. All rights reserved.
Printed in the United States of America.

No part of this book may be used or reproduced in any manner without written permission from the publisher, except in context of reviews.

ISBN 978-0-9892759-8-9

This is a work of fiction. Any resemblances to actual persons, living or dead; events; or locales are coincidental.

Cover design by Natalya Balnova
Book design by Amber Morena

For my parents,
and my parents' parents

CONTENTS

MAN AND WIFE

REFUGEES
\\\\\\\\

WE'D BEEN SETTLED AT THE CAMP only a year, though Momma said it may as well have been forever. She missed having walls between us, a roof over her head, a rug beneath her feet. She missed her hair dryer and her washing machine, her flowerbeds and her blue-and-white collection of country dishes, handpicked piece by piece over a decade's worth of fleas and fairs and online bids—missed it right down to the gravy ladle. She even missed the way I stood in front of the open fridge, complaining we had nothing good to eat, when we did—we had grapes and yogurt and string cheese, plus a tub of whipped topping and a bottle of chocolate syrup to go with the vanilla ice cream in the freezer.

1

"Dill pickles, gherkins, bread and butter. Black olives, green, stuffed with garlic and blue cheese," she said, wiping the sweat off her forehead with a sigh. "To think we used to pour the brine out down the sink."

I handed her another set of Daddy's boxers, dripping wet, to hang up on the line that stretched between our tent and the neighbors'. She'd work herself up like this, listing it all, the mythical contents of some frosty fridge, until the pain that gnawed constant in our bellies yawned so wide in hers it came unhinged. Then it was my job to say the lentils and rice weren't so bad, and we were lucky to have them. And because on that morning's hike out to our plot on the outskirts of the camp we'd seen that our plants had sprouted up, I was now able to say, "And your garden, it's small, but it's going to be blowing up with veggies."

She clenched her teeth around a clothespin and reached for the next wet underthing. I was glad she didn't fight me because I would've had to add that we were lucky too for the sun that made her sweat, the rain that when it fell too hard flooded our platform tent and soaked the mats we slept on, since otherwise we couldn't spare our rations for watering. The spring before, her garden gave so many peas that when the zucchini came up with summer I was relieved—at first. Then I didn't mind when the patrol she shared with other growers lapsed overnight and we were raided, the squash showing up the next day at market and Daddy refusing to buy.

I didn't realize at the time—when, before the snows were set to fall, we packed what we could into the car and headed south, leaving everything else, our foreclosed house, our inground pool, her hair dryer, behind—how hopeful she must have been to have brought the seeds at all. Those tiny packets were one thing that fit easily in her dress pockets next to her jewelry when, more than half-way down the length of I-75, the gas stations ran out of gas and we had to leave the car behind too. I had just figured, after weeks of walking with the caravan with whom we'd fallen in had finally ended at the camp, that this was what she had been picturing all along, what she and Daddy had been pointing us toward from the start. Later they let out that it'd been Grandma's, the retirement community clear down where orange groves once had been, though she had told us not to come. Her friends had turned against each other for the strain their families were putting on their meager resources and space.

"I suppose it has nothing to do with the fact I can no longer pay my part," Daddy had grumbled. "I suppose Patty would be welcome for her steady twenty percent— of course *she's* still got her house."

Patty was Daddy's older sister who lived modestly in a small desert city off a tenured teacher's salary. Grandma now mostly paid for herself, from Grandpa's pension and insurance. It was terrible to rely on her having another stroke before she could go broke.

All her life Aunt Patty had scrimped and saved, never investing in the market, never going on a trip, never put-ting in a lawn or pool—never even giving her body up to a husband and making kids, as Momma always pointed out. I was sad not to have cousins on top of no sister, and until the year past, it had seemed odd to live a life of deprivation when it was so easy to have one of plenty. Now I wondered why we hadn't been aiming the car west. I wondered if we would have then been stuck on the plains—or, if we had made it, whether Aunt Patty, after all the black sheep status she'd endured, would have answered the door. For my birthday, she used to send ten-dollar bills in one-dollar cards (the price printed right on back). Before that card even arrived in the mail, I'd have already charged to Momma's credit cards that much and more, in early presents to myself.

I remember tracing along the pattern of green, uttering the incantation *In God We Trust*. It seemed a relic both holy and base. Momma would snatch the ten away to hold it to the light, shaking her head. She'd thought cash was dirty, hated how it smelled.

Now in the patch that served as yard, where we sat the heat out and cooked meals on our handmade stove, Momma held herself in a wilting ghost of that proud posture: clipping up to the line the last of the wrung-out clothes we'd scrubbed clean in the basin. Once, her fingers had been manicured, had worn rings. Her hair, once smooth and blonde, was wound into a wiry bun, sparkled through with grays. When he didn't mind a swat on the backside, Daddy said when they first met he could never say no to her needs, for fear of hearing no back. Now he was just in the habit. Everything I'd once thought beautiful in her I'd realized was fake, and what was left, with her features stripped bare, just looked like me, only older.

She turned and brushed her hands against her shorts, cutoff khakis cuffed and soiled by blowing dirt. "I guess it's time you run off."

She said it wryly, sick of my company, but reluctant for me to leave. When chores were done, it left her little to do. She rarely sat with our neighbors, though she helped patrol their pot. Its scent drifted from their lean-to and stuck to our camp-issued sheets.

"You sure?" I asked. She waved me on, squatting down on the crate under the shade of the makeshift awning.

I slowly slinked out past our tent, rustling the plastic tarp, as if I were also reluctant to look for any joy. What I could never admit to her, what I could never squeeze in amidst complaints, was that I was happier here, with everything we had been worried over out of sight. The bills, I guess, were still coming, but we had no Internet access by which to view them, and the same went for our empty stock and bank accounts. The collectors, with our cell phones discarded, couldn't reach us. My last fall of school, the seventh grade, I'd started with no friends. Here I ran with a group of both girls and boys, barefoot, like we were still kids, not the pretend preening adults we'd been forced to become inside the halls of junior highs. I'd soon be graduating to ninth, had I access to a school realer than the one-room that Momma rarely bade me attend, since Daddy gave me lessons at night.

And then there was the stupid hope, the one I thought I held alone: when we'd first come over the rise and looked down on the camp—the shanties and the blue tarp tents that stretched for miles, the market block, the clinic and the school, the barbed wire all around—I'd blurted out in an awed whisper, "Do you think Sammie's here?"

Momma kept staring on ahead, her eyes so wide they watered, and Daddy answered, abrupt, "Highly unlikely." Meaning, despite its size, this could not be—considering what was happening in our country—the only camp of its kind, and probably also wanting not to get my or anyone's hopes up.

None of us had seen Sammie in over seven years, a span of time in which she'd undoubtedly grown into a different person. Momma had long since deleted and destroyed all her pictures, but I was sure I'd recognize the woman Sammie had become. She was the crucial step between us: shorter than Momma, taller than me, she'd have the same slim hips we had, the same flat chest, the set-back eyes, the narrow nose, the thin long lips—an overbite, since she'd refused braces, calling them, Momma said, prison bars, a racket. My own big sister, unlike Daddy's, who ran on lesson plans and ticking clocks, was transient, a runaway: a hopper of trains, turner of tricks—I'd pieced all this together from TV reports of other teenage runaways, as she had never sent an email or a postcard and had left her cell phone behind.

Daddy said it was chronic, her urge to bolt, something chemical in her blood sure as insanity. He'd seen it before in his family, his own dad, who left when Daddy was four. That's why Momma, when they met, liked him at once: he was used to women and their cloudy communication, their many needs.

Sammie ran twice, once at seven, before I was walking, and again at nine, when I was always throwing fits: first for an afternoon and then three days and nights. They'd found her in the woods, up a tree, eating nuts and berries. Now at fourteen, I was older than she'd been the third and final time she'd got away, but I felt nowhere near as old inside as she must've really been—technically not yet twelve years old—to leave and not return. How my parents knew she was alive was not explained, but somehow I knew it too. No body surfaced from the river, after all, and a tip or two got passed on to us from the Bureau—she was out there, an adult newly minted, and I had the feeling my whole life I'd never get caught up to her.

I didn't say it then, looking out at the camp that first time from the rise, I just thought it inside: now, finally, we had something in common. Now, we too, all four of us, were runaways.

I FOUND MY GANG IN A CIRCLE out back at the clinic. Hilary had just gotten out, cleared of her strep but still light-headed. She stepped back so I could join, and Mauricio kicked the sack to me. Darius, from the coast, had taught us hacky, a comeback sport that hadn't yet shown up in our landlocked towns. Daddy remembered it and laughed when I'd had Momma sew a fist of beans into a canvas ball. "Hang ten," he said. "Totally gnarly." I had no idea what he was talking about.

Momma didn't like my friends or how, she said, I was when I was with them. She meant behind her back, for the only evidence she had of my rising rebellion was how we all had made a style of our confines, showered in the camp showers less than we were allowed, let our hair go matted and gnarled, didn't let our mothers mend our clothes. It felt cool and easy not to care.

"We almost had to roll over to school without you," said Darius, catching the sack on his toes. But there seemed to be no rush; he thwacked it into the center.

"I had to help my ma." They all knew what she didn't, that I was her little girl even when she was out of sight, even in my oily, tangled hair, my loose dress with the tear across the stomach. I glanced over the sky. "What's up? It's after three."

"There's some new guru," Mauricio said disgustedly. "Fatima wants to go."

Fatima shrugged, talking around a candy disk held on her tongue. Her mother rarely traded wisely at market, and that was the way Fatima, who manned their budget, preferred it. "I heard he's cute. He's not even old. He's practically the same age as us."

Already my face was hot. Hilary caught my eye but looked away. I couldn't stand this kind of talk because it was a reminder that, beneath our games, Mauricio liked Fatima, and Hilary, Mauricio. Darius was gay, and maybe, or so I pretended, so was I. Hilary assumed this was a cover for my own crush on Mauricio. He wasn't even that cute, just had a broad chest and the beginnings of a moustache. If I'd had the choice, I'd rather Darius, with his smooth skin and gentle eyes, be into girls, but I knew that was a cop-out. He never would, and really, I just wanted us to keep these longings tamped because I saw how their eruption could mean our collapse.

Of course, that was before I saw the guru for myself.

THE SCHOOLROOM ALWAYS OPENED WIDE its windows and doors, which never helped the heat. The space was tight with tidy rows of little desks with seats attached, but by now the other kids had all gone home to see to chores. A sprinkling of adults, elder and middle-aged, sat in back or to the sides, noncommittal. Fatima wanted to sit up front, so Hilary followed after Mauricio. Darius and I sat behind, seeing how softly we could blow their necks before they noticed.

We saw no reason to be serious. Gurus mostly went from camp to camp, and some arose within our own, the conditions giving rise to a strange hope or premonitions, and people mostly heard them out out of politeness or a sense of hospitality. If the sermons persisted, too long for one sitting or too often in the week, their audiences petered off, and the guru took the hint, moving on to spread the gospel to another camp. Everyone else who felt a hole and sought to fill it with spirituality attended an allotted slot on Sundays: Muslims at dawn, Christians at noon, and Jews at sundown, with nondenominational meditation in between. And at the camp, that was most everyone, even those with only the vaguest of religious leanings. Sometimes Daddy and I went to meditation. Momma preferred to, in Daddy's words, luxuriate in her boredom.

Darius leaned in, grasping my wrist, so we could sync

our blows to go at once. Finally, Fatima snapped, whirling around to screech, "Would you suckers please act more legit?" and that was when the guru entered, a guitar slung on his back. He was slim and had long hair, eyes more beautiful than a woman's, and a man's strong jaw. He smiled at Fatima, and my face got hotter and hotter.

"Greetings, suckers," he said, and the adults politely laughed. He could've been anywhere between eighteen and thirty-three. He had an ageless voice, confident and calm. Darius dropped my wrist, staring. We were both of us, plus Hilary and Fatima too, feeling the same thing. Crossing his arms, Mauricio slumped in his seat.

He said his name was Steven and went immediately into a song, sitting cross-legged atop the teacher's desk and strumming the strings with his fingers. His singing voice was like his speaking one. It compelled you to listen. The chords led his range high and low, sounding now rough and graveled, now pure and nearly female. His eyelids relaxed so that it seemed he'd forgotten about us, had only to convince himself.

At first we were all embarrassed, it was so intimate to hear him play, especially with his eyes closed, but then we relaxed under his spell. There was a group of kids in camp who banged on buckets, and lots of people sang, while they worked, while they walked, while they sat around, but it wasn't often that we heard real music. And this wasn't a hymn or a hypnotic chant, as another guru might have done, but a melancholy original I could've heard on the radio, on one of Daddy's satellite stations he used to voice-command in the car. The lyrics told a story of an Old West woman in love, packing linens and clothes in her trousseau. These were stolen on the trail, her husband shot and their ox drowned. There seemed to be no moral. He ended with a slap to stop the strings. I hadn't realized, but I'd closed my eyes too. He set his guitar to the side, and his sermon began.

All the gurus I'd ever heard strode and swept their gaze around as they spoke of how what was lost to us was going to be returned. In the afterlife, right here in our new post-society, if we loved enough, prayed enough, worshipped him or her, lifted up our kin and ourselves. We could earn it back, build it again. This guru, Steven, lit on each of us in turn from his spot on the desk and said where we were was good for us. Desire bred desire, and if we kept chasing it, trying to hold what could not be held, we'd never be satisfied. We would build back up only to fail and fall again. We'd keep feeling alone.

"Do you truly feel you have nothing? Do you truly feel you no longer know yourself? Or do you know yourself better? Do you know your neighbors better? Do you have *more* than you can touch?"

He met my eyes, and I tingled, as with a fever, hot and cold. I felt infected, but my body wasn't treating the virus like a germ. Its spreading lifted me upright in my chair, while my face fell, shy and ashamed. Mauricio turned and scowled, as from the blows of my breath. Darius, who never tried to draw attention, raised his hand to volunteer himself, to say yes.

Even the adults perked up, nodding and murmuring. When it was done, the oldest woman and the youngest man, the hardest in any room to impress, each went to shake his hand. Hilary tried to hide it, but she was crying. Her family had had two pools, one outside and one in, a Jacuzzi.

ALL THROUGH THE MARKET, Fatima wouldn't stop gushing. "You see those lashes? I would kill for those eyebrows. And his nose, I wanted to lick it."

Her unabashed desire made mine smaller and smaller, until it was almost lost, then Hilary took our hands and quietly held them, sweaty and swinging, to stop us separating in the crowd. Darius nudged alongside, pressing me for an opinion.

"He's cute," I said simply, tamping the tingly warmth, and Hilary smiled at me.

"For a guy, you mean!" Fatima screeched. "Bet he could even turn Mauricio!"

We laughed, his face flaming from her attention as much as in defense.

With dinner on the horizon, the street was thick and close with the pushing and yelling of people buying-selling-trading. The accents were coastal, Northeastern, and, like mine, Middle West, with very few sounding Appalachian or of the South. We'd been displaced. We were in it—this camp, our titillation from this guru—together. The sun was high with no sense of waning, flies buzzing, dirt kicking up to coat our bare feet. A skinny dog darted between our legs, his tail brushing against me. I felt already that Momma had to meet Steven.

Nobody noticed Mauricio had fallen behind, but when he caught back up, he was holding a cup of ice he'd purchased from a vendor. "Ladies?" he offered.

Darius scowled. "Boy, we don't want that shit. We're *suffering*." He always did that, made light of what he sincerely believed.

Mauricio lunged as though to dump the cup out on his head, but Fatima, shrieking, held him back. She plucked out a melting cube and dotted it to her temples, drew it over her lips. Mauricio watched, Hilary watching him. We sucked ice all the way back to our sector and parted with a group hug for our tents. I was nervous to go home. I felt I was no longer the same self inside as I had been. It wasn't just the way the guru looked but how he'd been and what he'd said that, like foreign cells or oxygen, were coursing through my body.

Out back Momma was still sitting on her crate, Daddy hunched at the stove, stirring the lentils and rice. He seemed in good humor. She must've told him of the garden sprouting up, as he was saying, "How long before we see some greens?"

"You tell me," Momma said sullenly, squeezing the tension from her neck, her constant self-massage. All day Daddy scoured the countryside for work. Sometimes he came home with dollar bills, a jug of milk, an aching back. Today, I saw, he'd brought nothing. I hugged him from behind.

"Munchkin!" He turned with a grin from my embrace. "What sort of mischief have you been up to?"

I didn't know how to convince Momma about Steven.

I had to be sly to not suggest it outright. That always shut her down. She liked to have her own ideas. As Daddy dished out dinner from the pot, I rambled on. "He seems so familiar. He's just that kind of person. Like you've seen him before on TV."

"He sounds like a regular Jesus," Daddy said. "Does he practice what he preaches? What makes his message different from any other old-time religion?"

Daddy was always pressing me to think things through logically and to build arguments through evidence. Yet I found Steven difficult to explain. "I don't know," I said. "You didn't raise me with anything."

"It sounds to me like the oldest story ever told," Momma finally said with disdain. "You like him."

"*Like* like?" Daddy teased. He used to tickle me, but now the only way he touched me first was to poke me in the side. I squirmed and felt my face, my ears, my tongue, even my toes, hot with the rush of blood.

"Well," Momma said. "This I have to see."

HE WAS SET TO SPEAK AGAIN the next morning, early, before school. I wanted to go, but Momma said somebody needed to hike out to the garden.

"Aren't they on patrol?" I motioned to the empty lean-to next door.

"Yes, but they're going to be high as kites. Just sit with it, pull out the weeds. We can't be taking chances at this crucial stage." I understood. She wanted to keep me from him until she could gauge the threat. But in my mind, I was already gone. I was packing my trousseau.

I brought with me the little hand fork for the weeds, but when I arrived—the sun high and scorching, muscles burning in my legs—I was listless. I sat beside the beds of dirt dotted in green with my back to the camp and stared out past the barbed wire off at the rise we had first summited a year before, the rise Daddy crossed over every morning and back again every night. Beyond it was the highway he hitchhiked, the farms he begged for work. Beyond that was the city, whose downtown streets, we knew from friends of Mauricio's older brother, were filled with prostitutes and men who'd rob your body blind.

Outside the camp, a wanderer would meet women worldly and worse. And even inside, I couldn't compete with a Fatima—girls with hips and breasts who knew how to prop them up to cut through ration lines and get away with giving nothing extra in return. Fatima had full, pillowy lips and knew how to suck a candy or a cube of ice. And she was smart, so smart she took over for the teacher whenever math was more than long division. With her around, anyone like her, Steven would never even see me.

Midafternoon, hunger gnawing my belly, I hiked back. On the street, I ran into Hilary, lugging two jugs home from the water point.

"You weren't there this morning," she said, setting them down and tucking back her hair. I realized she had combed it and it was down, not in her messy ponytail. "I thought for sure you would be."

"Yeah, my ma," I said in explanation. My knees and elbows were caked in dirt. If Steven practiced what he preached, he wouldn't care, but I spit on my fingers and rubbed at them anyway.

I was about to ask how it had gone, if Momma seemed to like him, when Hilary said, squinting off at the sun, "Mauricio's going to get fed up with Fatima. She's so in love with that guru."

I clutched the hand fork tight, my face drained pale. My heart hurt.

"When he does, I'm going to be there." She looked at me sidelong to see if I cared. "Can you keep it secret, or will you spill?"

"I like Darius," I said dully to the ground. Water had splashed over the dirt from the spigots of her jugs. When I glanced up, I saw she was disappointed. In trying to show I didn't care about Mauricio, I'd also stepped back from the guru, far from the truth.

"Is it okay if I tell Darius you like Mauricio?" I added as though it could give authenticity to my crush.

"Okay." She said it kindly, even though I could tell she didn't buy it. "But the buck stops there." She let me walk with her, balancing the jugs, steadied with one hand, on top our heads.

When I slipped in past the tarp, Momma wasn't on her crate or even lying down in the tent. I figured she was waiting in the ration line or using up some of our water on a shower. But then the voices of next door drifted in along with the reek of smoke. Their shift was up, patrol handed over to the next. Momma was with them. That was her laugh, tittering hysterically.

Daddy missed dinner, a good sign that he had lucked on a job. Momma ate ravenously, her eyes dilated wide. I was afraid to bring up Steven, in case I needed Daddy there to be rational, but that night, as I tried to sleep, the mat soaked flat with humidity, I heard them talking out back.

"She had a sex change," Momma whispered. "But it's Sammie all right. I can see her inside."

"You mean transgender," Daddy said. "Transsexual. Trans." He fell silent with his thinking and came back with, "So why wouldn't he just go by Sam?"

Momma was impatient. She spoke with the voice that said Daddy always thought too much, didn't go with his gut and do what it would take to bring home the bacon. "She did it so we wouldn't find her. But now he's come to us."

WITH DADDY LEAVING EARLY, returning late, for his new ongoing gig on a farm's daytime security, for days it was just Momma and me. At first she didn't speak to me of Steven, just started going to all of his presentations, even his informal talks on the market block, when someone stopped him with a question they had been too shy to ask before a group and then a small crowd gathered round. She didn't seem to care if I came along or to realize she hadn't told me why she was there. Together we sat or stood in back and lingered long after it was done, watching him sling his guitar over his back or, with the same slender guitarist's hands, select and pay for a package of tobacco.

He might've been about the same age as Sammie, and I felt sick to think my draw could've been incestuous. From our inconspicuous spot, beneath the awning of a stall, I studied him for the set-back eyes, the narrow nose, the mouth with the overbite and thin long lips. My stomach settled. He didn't have them. I tested her.

"Momma," I said, in the thinning street, "did you like what Steven said about approaching life with love, how in giving of ourselves, we receive?" The sentiment had made me nervous, sent through with chills. The trembling in Momma's lip had been the only give in her blank face.

"Interesting, wasn't it?" she said, taking stock of her bare fingers for broken nails. Her tone was one of suspicion but without the vitriol she employed when recounting fights with Sammie, fights I'd not been privy to, sent off to play. She remembered back-sass, never gratitude or contrition; I recalled only slamming doors. Were her hands the same as Steven's? I envisioned him strumming, setting on the bone-sharp shoulder of an old woman, bumping callused fists with a young man. No, hers were squatter, with broader palms. Daddy's had the crooked little fingers, like Sammie's, like mine.

Yet something about him still seemed familiar. Familiar, I thought, in the way of long-lost loves meeting for the first time in love songs. One minute he made my heart fill up, seeming in his speech to search for me, and in the next, discarding me for the sight of a wide-hipped woman, he made it empty. And this was from a distance. Imagine if he touched my hair, if he kissed me.

"You shouldn't be so obvious," she finally slipped, on a brisk walk home. "If he knows we know, we'll never find out what it is she wants to get out of this."

"Momma," I said, stopping short. "You don't really think that's Sammie."

"He looked me right in the eye." She glanced over and kept going. "He knows it's me."

I guess she thought I'd been too young when Sammie left to recognize her. The fear that froze me cold the night I'd overheard her and Daddy soon melted to a trickling, a new suspicion: her purported delusion was just another way to keep me close to her, away from Steven. She'd counted on the fact that I would eavesdrop, and now there was no getting rid of her.

With Momma always around, I felt I couldn't go be with my friends. Across the schoolroom one afternoon, Fatima rolled her eyes and Darius sadly shrugged. Soon as the sermon finished, Mauricio dragged Hilary over to approach him. Steven held them both by the shoulders, murmuring like they were confidants. Mauricio straightened up. Hilary grazed her hand across her own cheek.

"Momma," I said afterward. "Shouldn't you be spending more time with the garden?" Over the weekend she'd missed patrol, and someone snapped half our peas from the vine.

"Daddy checks it every morning," she said vacantly. Daddy was doing everything. The one thing Daddy hadn't done was go see Steven.

At last Momma rolled from her mat one night to intercept Daddy's tired slog home to the tent. We each had taken to sleeplessly waiting on his trudging steps, glad for the excuse of dark to turn our backs and take a break from each other. Out back I heard the brushing of their bodies coming to meet, and then the wetness of mouth opening to mouth. In an entire year of nights spent in the tent, I'd never caught them in such affections, only witnessed one-armed hugs and soundless pecks.

"Not now, not here," Daddy said low.

"Can I help it I'm *excited* Sammie's back?" Momma said. "I don't know why you're not. Always so quick before to take her back in your arms."

"I don't understand," he said levelly, "why she would come back as a man and then proceed to ignore us."

"Maybe for her own protection," Momma argued. "A woman traveling alone. Your farmwife doesn't feel safe in her big empty house with her husband at the plow. If protecting her is what's expending all your energy."

"The crops," said Daddy. "Just like you, or what you're *supposed* to do, I patrol the crops. But if it's really worth it to you for me to be out a day's pay, I'll take one off."

I curled happily into a ball as with a rustle of the stagnant air, Daddy slipped into the tent, turning his sheet down in slow-mo so as not to disturb me. Momma stayed out with the chirping crickets on her crate. He'd set her right—set both of us right. He hadn't been home for an evening lesson in weeks, and my body had been buzzing only with thoughts of Steven. Daddy's concrete calculations could bring me balance, give the ideals of reconciliations and acceptance some weight: his measuring out of lentils, the math problems he made of receipts.

The evening Daddy joined us, he strode right up to Steven and shook his hand without so much as a flinch. He tapped his feet to Steven's song, this one up-tempo and full of hope, and listened intently as Steven spoke, taking notes that filled the backs of receipt after market receipt.

"It isn't her, Daddy," I whispered afterward, with people milling. Rather than interrupting Daddy's review of his notes, Momma had stood to move closer to Steven and soak up more while she could.

"It seems unlikely," he agreed. He never took a hard line when it came to usurping Momma in front of me. "But he sure has the both of you convinced of something. I don't know that you've even left your minds open to being changed. It happens to the best of us. The heart messing with the brain. "

I reddened with indignance. Even back when Daddy feared saying no to Momma's needs, his brain noted the cost and sought out deals. Though they were inseparable, embodied in who he was, I was convinced the guru's looks weren't what convinced me of his theology. "What if I told you I don't even *like* boys."

Daddy raised his brows. "One daughter trading her gender, the other her god-given sexuality? Sometimes you're all a little too crazy for me."

Momma was at the edge of a small group surrounding Steven. I went to get her so we could leave.

"—basic health and quality of life," he was saying, the man who must have asked a question nodding and nodding. "But cosmetic orthopedics, plastic surgery? You'll pardon me if I agree and go so far as to say that even so-called medicine can be a racket."

Still in his seat, Daddy looked up from his notes. But he

didn't move except to slowly shake his head and carefully fold them away.

"Come on, Momma," I said. Daddy didn't seem to want to wade up front to say goodbye. Outside, he told Momma he'd have to see more of Steven to know for sure if she was right, but for now he had a job to do. She sulked as Daddy drilled me on vocabulary on our walk through the market. The words caught on the air, becoming flies that I waved away while straining to parse if those people in the paperback stall, fanning splayed books for a breeze, were talking about Steven. Unlike with the other gurus, Steven's audiences only grew, and at the same time, Sunday worshippers thinned at the school. Steven was so much more than fodder for a schoolgirl crush.

Maybe I recognized him not from TV but from a dream. A dream that flowed through us all, like a river, like the flooding rain that rose beneath our platforms while we slept: me and Momma, the old women and young men, Fatima, Darius, and Hilary. When we woke, we found more than a rippling reflection of the deepest of our commonalities. Steven stood behind us, separate and real.

But with Momma as Steven's shadow, forever lurking in between, I'd never get next to him. She kept bringing her darkness to his light.

"That house, that stuff—that was our love Sammie didn't want. He's doing this to hurt us, all this pretending, all this talk about how we deserve this camp, this filth, this poverty. When *she* was the selfish brat." She moved her hands in staggered gestures as she spoke, reached to squeeze the tension from her neck.

"But Momma." I struggled to keep up through the dusking street. Smoke streamed from the backs of shanties, the blue tarp tents. Someone was singing one of Steven's songs. Somebody laughed a snorting laugh. Somewhere, I smelled frying bacon. It made my stomach ache. "That's not what he's saying. Momma, if you're so sure he's Sammie—"

In the middle of her stride she stopped. She was yanking out her bun, gray wiry strands frizzing around her face. On her arm she slapped a mosquito.

"Momma?" I slowly came closer. She waved me on toward our sector. We had no streetlights in the camp for after the sun had set and I couldn't be sure, but it seemed her eyes had gone wide and watery in the dark. It reminded me of when, taking in the camp for the first time from the rise, she'd simply withstood, without acknowledgment, my hope for Sammie.

"Go on. Tell Daddy when he's home I'll be a little late. I'm going to the garden. Pick us some greens."

I walked until Momma dropped from sight, still standing in the street. I wandered through the blocks of different sectors, smelling the same kinds of smells, hearing the same kinds of talk, reconciled or strategizing, how to make do or get out. But since Steven had come, the bitterness had tapered off. People told more stories and jokes, the point of which were not that Things were better then, just simply, Remember when? Darius had told me where Steven slept, in a tent a young couple had given up to go stay in her parents' shanty. It was only temporary. The guru always left. I stood outside it. Inside I heard a woman crying. By the light of a kerosene lamp, I could see her outline, her form bowed over that of another, sitting upright. I lifted up the edge of the tarp.

Momma was at Steven's cross-legged feet, begging Sammie's forgiveness for what she'd failed to give. "Please, tell me, please," she was sobbing. "I don't know what it is."

Her tears were hysterical, same as her laugh. Both seemed so strange, I realized, because I rarely heard them. Steven wanly smiled and motioned for me to enter. My heart beat. I ducked under the tarp and knelt beside Momma on the platform floor of the tent. Close up, the lines on Steven's face revealed him to be older than I had thought. His eyes seemed viscous and warm, the skin around them crinkling. His age was not what began to make him feel forever lost to me, but it did set him farther away even as he was near.

"You want to find your sister?" he asked, in that lyrical, male-female voice. Momma was still crying. Maybe it drowned him out. Maybe, in the short time before I'd arrived, he'd tried to convince her he wasn't Sammie, and Momma just couldn't hear. She had done nothing to indicate that she realized I was there.

I nodded, a knot forming in my throat. He pointed to his chest, a dress shirt half unbuttoned with the pocket ripped from it. "You've got to strip yourself to nothing to find the part no one can take."

STEVEN LEFT IN THE NIGHT, taking with him Momma, one of the guns shared on patrol, and a few other women.

No one especially young or pretty—known, in fact, for being strange—and all, apparently, willing to go all the way. Not Hilary, not Fatima. With Darius and Mauricio, they came to me. We sat out back on the dirt while Daddy went to the clinic to make some calls—to the farmhouse where he worked, to the police, insofar as they could help. Half the country had drifted from home.

"You were with them? What did he say?" Mauricio asked, unable to hide his glee.

"He told me he'd take care of her," I said emptily, "and in the morning everything would be okay."

"It's all right to cry," Fatima assured me. Mauricio had his hand on her thigh, and she wasn't pushing it away. Only Hilary was crying. I was dried out as a husk, wrung from my infection. Steven was a fool's-gold fake, and for him Momma had deserted me. He hadn't come to help us, only to collect odd jewels for the crown he'd wear best somewhere else, perhaps in search of more: brighter, stranger. Like us, he'd always want, just differently. As my friends walked off, Darius wrapped an arm around Hilary's waist. As though suddenly remembering not to forget about me, Darius called back, "See you soon, raccoon!"

That day Daddy and I sat in meditation for over an hour. The schoolroom wasn't crowded, its desks cleared out, but it would be for many Sundays to come. People came in droves; summoned by their need to fill the hole of our guru's departure, to slow the greedy pulsing of their blood, to sweat out their desire.

My mind wandered once to Sammie, whom—now that

I'd lost Momma—I understood I'd never known well enough to truly miss. The hole she'd made was vague: that of a big sister who'd always been closing her door. There had even been a part of me that was relieved when the discord in our family had been plucked out, as if by a surgery, the wound sewn shut and healed but for the scar, oddly neat for its concealing of a mystery. One day, about a week before she ran for good, she'd dragged her toys and dolls out to the curb, dumping her computer tablet in its leather case, the patent leather shoes and crinkly tutus she'd never worn and Momma never handed down—emptied her room of most everything but her bed and trunk, too big to move. I'd gently cradled the doll with the long blonde curls, the blinking blue eyes and pale porcelain skin. "If you want it, you can have it," she'd said. "You can have it all." She said the same thing nights she missed dinner and I smuggled her dessert; neighbors noted her thinness: she seemed sick. Such gestures of hers were only in part of generosity; such displays not in self-lessness, but for the show. I just took that doll. I could picture it still sitting on my shelf back at the house, abandoned, its petticoat and bloomers ballooning out between its legs.

Then, never shifting from the lotus, I brought my focus back to the breath, in through my nose and out my mouth. Even if you did not know what to expect, you could learn to sit like this through anything.

We came out stiff from the school, into a gathering breeze. My limbs were light and buzzing in their loose dress, torn across the stomach, and Daddy seemed relieved of worries, at peace. The sky was going dim with gray-blue clouds rolling in.

"I've thought about it," I said at dinner, as it started to rain. We shared the crate under the awning and had our bowls in our laps. "The only way we're ever going to get out of here and make our way to Aunt Patty is if I come work with you. We can still do our lessons. Maybe on the road."

Daddy stopped chewing, looking troubled. He swallowed hard.

"You don't know what kind of help some men would want from you out there."

"You're wrong," I said. "I do."

MAN AND WIFE
\\\\\\\

THEY SAY EVERY GIRL REMEMBERS that special day when everything starts to change.

I was lying under the tree in my parents' backyard, an oak old enough to give shade but too young to be climbed, when Dad's car pulled into the garage. All afternoon I'd been riding bikes with Stacie, but we'd had a fight when she proposed we play in my basement—it *was* getting too hot out, but I was convinced she was only using me for my Barbies. This was eight years ago. I was nine and a half years old.

Dad came out and stood in the driveway, briefcase in hand, watching me pull up grass. "Mary Ellen!"

29

I yanked one final clump, root and dirt dangling from my hands, and sat up.

"Come inside. I have wonderful news."

In the kitchen Dad was embracing my mother, his arms around her small, apron-knotted waist. "I can't believe it went through," she was saying. She turned to me with shiny eyes, cleared her throat, and said in her sharp voice, "Mary, go get down the good glasses."

I pushed a chair to the cupboards and climbed onto the countertop. Two glass flutes for my parents and, for myself, a plastic version that I'd salvaged from last New Year's, the first time I'd been allowed, and encouraged, to stay up past midnight and had seen how close the early hours of the next day were to night.

Dad took down the last leftover bottle of champagne and popped it open, showering the kitchen floor. My mother laughed and wiped her hands on her polka-dotted apron, as if she'd gotten wet.

"Hold up your glass, Mary Ell," said Dad. He filled it halfway, and theirs to the rim. When in the past I'd been curious about alcohol, my parents had frowned, taken a drink, and feigned expressions of disgust. On New Year's, for instance, my cup had held plain orange juice, and the next morning, while my parents still slept, I'd had orange juice in it again.

"A toast." My mother held up her glass and waited.

I waited too. The champagne fizzed, bubbles rising.

"To Mary," said Dad, and then he stopped, choked up.

"Our own little girl, to be a woman," my mother said. "Bottoms up."

They clinked their glasses together, and mine met theirs dully, with a tap that brought an end to the pleasant ringing they'd created. I brought the champagne to my lips. I found that, if ingested in small sips, it was quite drinkable, no worse than my mother's Diet Coke, and it had the welcome effect of making me feel I was floating away.

"Don't you want to hear what the big news is?" said Dad. My mother turned her back on us to the cutting board, where she was chopping a fresh salad.

In a small voice I said, "Yes." I tried to smile, but that feeling was in my stomach, made more fluttery by drink. I recognize the feeling now as a kind of knowledge.

"Well, do you remember Mr. Middleton? From Mommy and Daddy's New Year's party?"

At the party I'd been positioned, in scratchy lace tights and a crinoline-skirted dress, at the punch bowl to ladle mimosas for their guests. Many of their friends introduced themselves to me that night: Mr. Baker, Mr. Silverstein, Mr. Weir. Some bent to my height and shook my hand. Mr. Woodward scolded me for insufficiently filling his cup, and his young wife, Esmerelda, my former babysitter, led him away.

"Mr. Middleton—that nice man with the moustache? You talked together for quite some time."

Then I remembered. As I served other guests, he lingered with a glass of sweating ice water, talking about his business. He directed his words to the entire room, looking out over it rather than at me, but he spoke quietly, so only I could hear. He offered figures: annual revenue, percentages, the number of loyal clients. And then: "My business is everything. It is my whole life." I looked up at him curiously, and his face reddened; his moustache twitched. When he finally left, patting my shoulder and thanking me for indulging him, I was relieved. I'd had little to say in return—no adult had ever spoken to me that way—and I'd felt the whole time, on the tip of my tongue, the remark that might have satisfied and gotten rid of him sooner.

"That's the good news," Dad said. "He's gone ahead and asked for your hand. And we've agreed to it."

My mother put down the knife and finished off her champagne. I wanted no more of mine.

"Well, don't be so excited," said Dad. "Do you understand what I'm saying? You're going to be a wife. You're going to live with Mr. Middleton, and he's going to take care of you, for the rest of your life. And, one day, when we're very old, he'll help out your mother and me too."

"Yep." He smiled. "It's all settled. Just signed the contract this afternoon. You'll really like him, I think. Nice man. You seemed to like him at the party, anyhow."

"He was okay," I managed. It was as I'd feared, somewhere, all along: the toast, the party, everything. But now he had a face, and a name. Now it was real: my future was just the same as any other girl's. Yet none of my friends had become wives yet, and it didn't seem fair that I should be the first taken. For one thing, I was too skinny. They say men first look for strength in a wife. Next they look for beauty, and even with braces and glasses yet to come, I was a homely little girl. It's last that men look for brains. You may notice that I skipped over wealth. While rumors of sex spread freely at school, it wasn't clear to me then just how money fit in. It was discussed only in negotiations, when lawyers were present and we were not. It was best that way, for our parents, who tried to keep such things separate. A girl shouldn't have to worry over what a number said of her promise or worth.

At dinner I pushed the food around on my plate, clearing a fork-wide path and uncovering the blue-and-white pattern of little people kneeling in rice fields and pushing carts. My mother was on her third glass of champagne—she wouldn't last through *Jeopardy!*—and she was laughing at everything Dad said about his anxious day at the office.

A timer buzzed, and my mother rose from the table to pull out her raspberry pie. She approached me with the dish clasped in her oven mitts.

"Take a good look at that pie, Mary."

The crust was golden brown, its edges pressed with the evenly spaced marks of a fork prong. Sweet red berries seeped through the three slits of a knife.

"It's perfect," she said, with her usual ferocity.

THE NEXT MORNING STACIE ACTED like our fight hadn't happened, and I wanted to play along. We went to ride bikes while my mother showered. Dad's car had left already for work, and the garbage can had been dragged out to the curb. The champagne bottle poked from the recycling bin, ready to be taken away. It was another summer day.

"We had a celebration last night," I told Stacie. "Dad let me have booze."

"Oh, yeah? What for?" She pedaled ahead and moved onto the street, which her parents, and mine, forbade.

I had to shout, she was so far ahead. "Someone named Mr. Middleton wants to take me."

Stacie slammed on her brakes and turned her bike to face me. Once caught up, I kept going.

"When?" she demanded, appearing alongside. "You know he can't take you yet."

"Why not?" I said, but I assumed, as did Stacie, that there'd be a long period of engagement. In the fall we were to start the fifth grade, and it was rare for a girl still in elementary to be taken.

"He must really like you," Stacie said, in awe. We pedaled slowly, pensively. "But you're so skinny."

Mrs. Calderón, in her silken robe, was out watering her rose bushes. She waved.

"We'd better get on the sidewalk," I said.

When we reached Maple Court, we laid our bikes on the island and sprawled in the warm grass, making daisy chains from the flowering weeds. Stacie put her hand on my arm. It was rare for us to touch.

"Whatever happens," she said, "don't dump me."

"What do you mean?"

"I mean, ever since my sister went to live with Mr. Gordon, she never plays with me anymore. When she comes over, she just sits in the kitchen with my mom drinking tea." She rolled her eyes. "They talk about recipes, and my mom gives her a frozen casserole that she pretends to Mr. Gordon she made by herself."

"Okay," I said. "I promise."

She held up her pinky, and I joined it with mine.

"I promise, when I live with Mr. Middleton, you can still come over and play Barbies."

"Not just Barbies," she said. "We'll still play everything. We'll still be best friends."

I hadn't even been sure we were best friends, since during school she spent her time with ratty-haired Cassandra and I, in protest, with the studious Chan twins. But I remained solemn. Maybe she wasn't using me. Besides, although I couldn't really imagine what it would be like to be a wife, I knew I wouldn't want to be stuck with Mr. Middleton all the time. I began to laugh.

"What?"

"He has the stupidest moustache!" I drew a thin line above my mouth with my finger, sweeping up at the edges to indicate the way it curled.

"Probably, you can make him shave it off. My sister makes Mr. Gordon wear socks all the time, so she doesn't have to see his feet."

Stacie picked apart her chain and let the flowered weeds fall—she had a theory they could again take root. I wore mine around my wrist but lost it during the ride back. My mother was still in the bathroom, the mingled scent of her products floating out beneath the door.

AFTER SERVING US TUNA-AND-PICKLE SANDWICHES, my mother sent Stacie home.

"But why?"

"Shhh," she said. "I need to talk to you."

I folded my arms across my chest and glared at her.

"Don't," she said. "Just don't. Come here with me."

In the living room, she sat and patted the couch beside her. The television wasn't on, which made the room feel too still and too quiet, like nothing happened in it when we weren't around.

"Now, I know Daddy explained that you're going to be a wife. But do you know what that means?"

I refused to look at her, though I could feel her eyes on my face. "Yeah. I'll go live with Mr. Middleton. I'll have to make him dinner."

"Yes," she said. "But you'll have to do more than that."

"Can I still play Barbies with Stacie? I promised her."

"You did, did you."

I nodded. I told my mother everything that Stacie had said. It made me proud that she was jealous, and I thought it would make my mother proud too.

"I'm sorry to say, it's really up to Mr. Middleton when, and if, you can play with your friends. And he may not appreciate you, still just a little girl, telling him to shave off his moustache. He's had that thing for years." She halted a creeping smile. "What I'm trying to say is, you'll belong to him. You'll have to be very obedient—not that you haven't always been a good girl. Your father and I are very proud of you. You get such good grades and stay out of trouble."

She paused, frowning. "I don't think you realize just how lucky you are that Mr. Middleton has offered to take you. He's a very successful man, and he's made quite a generous offer, for little in return." She patted my leg. "I don't mean you, of course. Any man would be lucky to have you. But to be honest, I'm not sure why he's so eager to settle it."

I stared at the black television screen. "Can I go to Stacie's now?"

"Wait. We're not through." She stood and approached the bookshelf. On days when I stayed home sick, I'd lie on the couch and stare at that bookshelf. Each book's spine, its title and design, suggested something of its story, and their order and arrangement seemed fixed, like the sequencing of photographs along the hallway wall: from my parents' wedding—my mother thirteen and Dad twenty-seven—to the day of my birth to my fourth-grade class picture. But as my mother took out the Bible and a few romance paperbacks, I saw that behind them were more books, a whole hidden row, the shelf deeper than I'd realized. She removed from hiding a slim volume called *Your Womanly Body*, its cover decorated in butterflies and soft-colored cut flowers blooming in vases.

"This will tell you *some* of what you need to know about being a wife. I imagine Mr. Middleton won't expect much from you at first. After all, you're still very young."

I began to turn the pages: there were cartoons of short and tall and skinny and fat women, their breasts different sizes and weights, with varying colors and masses of hair between their legs. The pictures weren't a shock to me. I'd seen my mother naked before, and Stacie had confirmed that her own looked much the same. Once I'd even seen Dad, when I surprised him by waiting outside the bathroom door for a Dixie cup of water late one night.

"You'll have a child someday, of course. But most people like to wait until they're older and know each other better. I, for instance, had you when I was eighteen. By today's standards, that's still a little young.

"It can be scary, at first." My mother's voice had turned soft, and she was staring out the window at the tree. "The important thing to remember is, even though he's in charge, you can have some control. Pay close attention: what he wants the most may be very small, and you can wait out the rest."

I already knew there were ways to put off sex: some girls "sucked" their husbands "off," others cried until left alone. And if a girl did become pregnant too soon, if it would be unseemly for her to keep the baby, I knew there were ways to get rid of it. But still, I'd rather not think about all that before I had to face it.

My mother was saying, "A man's life is spent waiting and preparing for the right girl. It can be very lonely. In a way, girls have it easy—"

"Mommy, when will I go live with Mr. Middleton?"

"I was getting to that, Mary. You can be so impatient." She lifted the book from my hands and turned to put it away. "You'll be going to him in the fall."

"Oh." I stared down at my bare summer feet, callused, tan, and dirty. "After school starts?"

"Mary. There'll be no school for you this fall. You'll have a house to take over."

The feeling was back in my stomach, more of an ache now, and all I wanted was to curl up on the couch while my mother brought Jell-O and chicken noodle soup. On sick days you could escape the movement of the world. It was always difficult to get back into it, to catch up on schoolwork and eat real food again, but this time I wasn't sure I ever wanted to rejoin the world.

Yet the books were different now, forming a front all lined up: decoys as much as fonts of knowledge. I wouldn't be able to not think about that.

"Of course, he'll probably let you go back soon. He'll want you to. That's what Mr. Middleton told us—that he admired your mind. He said he could tell you're a very bright girl.

"I should be so lucky," she added darkly. "Your father only saw my strength."

IT BECAME ROUTINE FOR MR. MIDDLETON to spend Sunday afternoons with us. At dawn my mother yanked open all the blinds, and the acrid smells of housecleaning began to fill the rooms. Even Dad was kept from sleeping in and given chores to do. I was ushered straight into the kitchen: "Do me one little favor," she said.

"Knead this dough. No, like this. Punch it, like you're pissed off.

"Check the stove. Has it reached the preheated temperature? Well, is it hot?

"Okay, now we'll let that marinate. You know what's in this marinade? Just smell it—what does it smell like?"

Once I had completed my mother's "favor" ("Umm, it smells sweet" "Good! That's the honey"), I snuck out while her back was turned.

I was to be scrubbed "my pinkest" in the shower. She showed me how to use Q-tips to clean out my ears, to rub lotion over my skin, and to pluck the little hairs I hadn't noticed before from between my eyebrows. She swore under her breath when she nicked me with the pink disposable razor—my legs slathered in a thick gel that smelled like baby powder. "Here," she said. "You finish."

I slid the blade along my leg, pressing as lightly as possible.

I was to wear "one of my prettiest dresses," which meant that I rotated between the three in my closet. Their straps dug into my shoulders, their crinoline scratched my bare legs. The first Sunday, my mother threw onto my bed a package from Sears. Inside were three training bras. I didn't have anything resembling breasts, and when I finally did, years into my marriage, they were so small that I continued to wear the trainers for some time. My husband didn't seem to care or know the difference.

Every Sunday had the feel of a holiday—the boredom of waiting for the guest to arrive and the impatience of waiting for him to leave. Mr. Middleton always brought a bouquet of flowers, at the sight of which I was to feign surprise and gratitude. Every week, the same supermarket assortment of wildflowers that smelled rank and bitter, like weeds. Mr. Middleton sat with my father in the living room while I trimmed and arranged the flowers in my mother's crystal vase. She had me stir something or taste it for salt before nudging me back out to join them.

Mr. Middleton would wear a full suit and tie, despite the fact that our house had no air conditioning. As the afternoon wore on, he would take off the suit jacket, loosen and remove the tie, roll up the sleeves of the dress shirt, and, lastly, undo the shirt's top button, revealing a tuft of dark curly hair. The hair on his head was straight, and he'd run a hand through it, slicking it back with his sweat. Dad, in a short-sleeved polo shirt and khaki shorts, would watch, smiling to himself. My shaven skin felt cool and smooth. I had to stop myself from running my hands along my legs as I sat listening to them talk "business." Their tone was cordial, yet they seemed to eye each other warily. I didn't consider it then, but Dad was likely sensitive to the fact that while he had to report to a boss, Mr. Middleton was his own.

"How's business?"

"Business is good. You?"

"Business is good. Clients?"

"Clients are good. Got to treat them right, keep them happy," Dad said.

"Of course."

In and out of the room bustled my mother. She refilled the pitcher of lemonade, replenished the dish of melting ice cubes, brought out bowls of mixed nuts and pretzels and onion dip. Before long, this became my job. I'd stand before Mr. Middleton with a tray of pickles and olives.

"Hmm, let's see." He'd mull over the choices, select a pimento-stuffed green olive. I'd turn to offer the tray to Dad, who had a penchant for sweet pickles, but then: "Please, wait just a moment—perhaps another. Hmm, let's see." And he'd choose a kalamata. The metal tray was heavy, but my arms grew stronger, and I learned to balance it on my shoulder.

Mr. Middleton rarely addressed me directly. Which

is not to say he wasn't speaking to me. "Profit margins" and "quarterly analyses" were discussed with glances and smiles in my direction. But he never asked what I thought, how I was doing, how I had spent my week. Adults, I knew, just liked to humor children, and ordinarily those questions tired me, causing me to clam up on the pretense of feeling shy. But in this situation it was disconcerting. After all, wasn't Mr. Middleton supposed to like me? What were we going to say to each other when we were, one day, inevitably, alone? I knew I would be expected to say something; wives, especially as they grew up, didn't have to be invited to speak. They scolded their husbands for things they were doing wrong, or weren't doing at all. They had stories to tell, of what had happened that day at the supermarket, of the rude cashier and the unmarked price of the fresh loaf of bread.

For the time being, I followed my mother's advice the best I could. I wouldn't speak unless spoken to. I sat up straight in the chair, didn't complain if the food at dinner was strange, didn't ask to turn on the television. I paid close attention to Mr. Middleton; I focused on his moustache, the way it moved with his mouth; studied the shine of his gold watch; viewed the gradual stripping of clothing, the sweat gathering on his forehead and alongside his nose, where his glasses slid. I may have already been following my mother's advice, but I don't remember thinking so. I never liked to admit I was doing as she suggested. I preferred to credit my own volition.

Mr. Middleton seemed to me older than my father, though he was almost a decade younger. Dad was strict, but he could be silly, wasn't afraid to be lazy, and had been known to watch cartoons that even I found stupid. Mr. Middleton was too polite and too proper. He was boring in the way a robot would be: never leaving to go to the bathroom, never saying anything Dad disagreed with or found ridiculous. They would have had much to argue about—they do now—their strategies in business so different: Dad doting on his clients, trying to keep them pleased each step of the way; Mr. Middleton acting with cool aggression against their wishes, with the long run in mind, the biggest possible profit. I suppose we were all on our best behavior.

By dinnertime the business talk had faltered, and the men punctuated their silence with compliments for the meal—something Dad never did when it was just the three of us. This was when my mother took over. "Thank you," she might say. "Mary Ellen helped prepare that."

"Did she? It's quite good," said Mr. Middleton.

"Oh, she's learning. Believe it or not, just a month ago even something this simple would have been beyond her."

Mr. Middleton smiled politely and chewed, his moustache moving up and down, a piece of couscous caught in the right-side curl.

"There is still so much for her to learn, I'm afraid. You mustn't—you mustn't expect too much, from the start."

"But of course Donna will get her up to speed," said Dad. "Won't you, honey?"

"Of course," my mother said. "All I meant was, Mary is such a fast learner. Why, just the other day the sauce was starting to stick, and instead of letting it burn or calling me, she just turned down the burner and gave it a stir. How about that?"

The heat from the kitchen was creeping into the dining room, and a bead of sweat slipped down Mr. Middleton's forehead. His top button, at that point, remained done. He offered nothing but another polite smile. Maliciously I wanted to call attention, in front of everyone, to the cous-cous still in his moustache. "Right there," I'd interrupt, pointing to a spot above my own lip. This was something a wife could do, scold or embarrass her husband for his own good. But I knew I hadn't earned it yet, and it would take years of waiting, quietly noting.

Mr. Middleton seemed oblivious to my parents' fears and cover-ups, but I've come to see that he was not, nor did he suffer them in silence purely out of politeness. I can look back now with some sympathy. I can see myself in him: he was determined to behave in the way that was expected, in the belief, often false but sometimes accurate, that this gave him some autonomy. And after all, he was getting what he wanted.

ONE SATURDAY AFTERNOON Mr. Middleton showed up while my parents were out. They were leaving me home alone more often in preparation for the days when I'd be keeping house, with Mr. Middleton off at work. Usually I found myself frozen, unable to act as I would if my parents were around. I had a great fear of doing something wrong, either accidentally (opening the door to a danger-ous stranger or coming upon some matches, which would inadvertently scratch against something and become lit, igniting a raging fire) or purposely, overcome by the thrill of risk. The only way to ensure this wouldn't happen was to remain on the couch until they came back.

At the sound of a knock at the door, I lifted a slat of blind and peered out at Mr. Middleton: no flowers in hand, no suit and tie. He wore blue jeans and sports sandals, a polo shirt like those Dad owned. His arms were covered in those dark, curly hairs. Through the peephole, his nose was made long by the curved glass, and his moustache twitched nervously. It gave me a small thrill, making him wait. Just as he began to back away, I did as I should and opened the door.

"Mary Ellen. What a pleasant surprise."

"Hello," I said politely. "Would you like to come in?"

He looked down the block, both ways. It was quiet for a Saturday. Only Mrs. Calderón was out, pruning her blooming roses. She'd recently explained to me that she had to cut them back so they could grow. Mr. Middleton smiled in her direction and entered the house.

"I'm home alone," I said. It seemed best if I made that clear right away.

"I won't stay long. You see, I was just in the neighborhood and thought I'd drop by."

That was reasonable to me, but it seemed out of character for Mr. Middleton, who operated purely, I thought, on formality and routine. "Would you like a glass of iced tea with lemon?" I asked.

"No, thank you."

He wasn't sitting, so I didn't sit, unaware that I might

have offered him a seat. The expression on his face was, as always, neutral, and he didn't return my stare. I felt I was doing something grossly wrong—I was still unfit to be a wife, unable to handle company on my own. My mother would scold me if she knew I'd received him in a T-shirt from last year's spelling bee and purple shorts stained with Kool-Aid.

I tried again. "How's business?"

He smiled and lowered himself to my height, his hands coming to rest on his knees. "Very well, thank you," he said. "But today, you see, I was thinking of you. I thought you might like to show me your Barbies."

No adult had ever asked to see them, and, to my knowledge, they'd never been mentioned in his presence. My mother allowed no visitors, other than my friends, into the basement. She had warned me that the Barbies would have to go when I went to Mr. Middleton. To head off my tears, Dad had added quietly that perhaps, for a while, they could leave them set up in the basement for when I came to visit.

I watched for some sign in Mr. Middleton that he was joking or only humoring me, but he reached out a hairy arm and took my hand. His wasn't sweaty, though the day was muggy and humid, and his skin was surprisingly soft. On the narrow stairway he didn't let go; my arm strained and pulled behind me as I led him into the basement. His knees cracked as he took the stairs.

The basement was unfinished, just hard tiles, exposed beams, and many-legged insects. Stacie complained about the centipedes, but they appeared less often than the spiders. Strips of sunlight came in through the windows along the driveway, where you could see feet pass on their way to the side door.

Mr. Middleton dropped my hand and approached the Barbies' houses slowly, as if in awe. The toys sprawled from one corner of the room to the other, threatening to take over even the laundry area; the foldout couch, which I maintained took up valuable space, sometimes served as a mountain the Barbies visited in the camper. There was one real Barbie house, pink and plastic; it had come with an elevator that would stick in the shaft, so I had converted the elevator to a bed. The other Barbie home was made of boxes and old bathroom rugs meant to designate rooms and divisions; this was the one Stacie used for her family. The objects in the houses were a mixture of real Barbie toys and other adapted items: small beads served as food; my mother's discarded tampon applicators were the legs of a cardboard table. On a Kleenex box my Barbie slept sideways, facing Ken's back; both were shirtless, her plastic breasts against him.

Mr. Middleton asked about the construction and decoration of the rooms. He said he admired my reuse of materials. "A creative way to cut costs," he noted.

I shrugged. "Mom and Dad won't buy me anything else."

He nodded thoughtfully. "You work well within limits."

"I guess," I said, but I was pleased. He was admiring my mind.

"Well, you have quite a talent for design—I've seen

professional blueprints more flawed." He suggested that in the future we might have a home built, one I could help plan.

Then he leaned down and stroked Barbie's back with his index finger. "Do they always sleep this way?" he asked.

I blushed and only shook my head. Sometimes they lay entirely naked, as my parents slept. Sometimes Barbie slept on top of Ken, or vice versa.

"Can you show me another way they might sleep?" he asked.

I hesitated, then picked up the dolls and put their arms around each other's bodies in a rigid hug. I tilted Barbie's head and pressed her face against Ken's, as if they were kissing, and laid them back atop the Kleenex box. Mr. Middleton watched with his detached interest.

"Your Barbies must love each other very much," he observed.

I'd never really thought about it that way. They were just doing what my parents and people on television did because they were married. But sometimes, when I was alone, it gave me that fluttery, almost sick feeling deep in my stomach, and I took the dolls apart.

Mr. Middleton stood and turned away. He held up his wrist to a sun strip, examining his watch, for what seemed a long time. "Well, thank you for sharing them with me. But I should be on my way."

I nodded, then recovered my manners. "Can I walk you to the door?"

"No, thank you, Mary Ellen. I'll show myself out."

On Sundays he'd shake my parents' hands before he left, and now I wondered if I should offer mine. But instead he reached out and patted me on the head, once, twice, then the last time just smoothing my hair, as my mother would to fix a stray strand, but much gentler.

When I heard the front door close, I knelt in front of the Barbie house. It was difficult, as my Ken's arms were straight, not bent like some, but I moved his arm so that it stroked Barbie's back. I startled when my mother called from the top of the stairs. I hadn't seen feet in the windows or heard a key in the door.

I didn't tell them that Mr. Middleton had been over, and the next day when he came for Sunday dinner, he didn't mention it either. It didn't occur to me until years later that the whole thing might have been prearranged. I could find out now; Mr. Middleton tells me anything I ask. He may tease, but he knows when to stop. It's quite possible he's even learned to fear me. For all his skill in the world of business, I think he understands less about the world without than I do.

THAT SEPTEMBER, with Stacie back at school, my days were spent alone with my mother. She was nervous about the upcoming ceremony and would sit with me at the kitchen table for hours with catalogues of flowers and dresses.

"Do you like these roses? Or something more unique—orchids? But so expensive."

I would shrug. "It doesn't matter."

Depending on her mood, she would either become angry ("If it doesn't matter to you, who does it matter to? Pick out some flowers!") or take my reticence as deference to what she thought was best ("The orchids are lovely, but we'd best be practical, hmm?").

Once, paging together through pictures of dresses, she became so frustrated with me that she disappeared into the bathroom for almost an hour. Finally I knocked on the door. "Mommy? I left it open to the one I like." I heard water running, and when she came out, she caught me around the shoulders and held me against her, my face nuzzling her stomach. "That's my good girl," she whispered above my head.

One afternoon was spent sewing, another polishing silver. The cooking lessons took on new vigor, and she had me reducing wine-based sauces, braising meats, and chopping fresh herbs for most of the day. Dad would come home, see everything that had been set out on the table and everything that still simmered on the stove and roasted in the oven, throw his hands up in the air, and say, "I don't know how you expect us to consume all this, Donna. Maybe you could lay off her a bit." But then he'd sit down and attack the food with an appetite that had the air of duty, sighing and unbuttoning his pants for dessert.

Stacie came over after school a couple of times a week, but she brought Cassandra; the Chan twins had forsaken me, believing my imminent wifehood to have changed me already. With only two Barbie houses, Stacie, Cassandra, and I couldn't play together fairly. Besides, I didn't want Cassandra and her ratty hair anywhere near them. Instead we sat on the porch eating gingersnaps—just talking and not playing anything. Other girls who'd been promised spent their time in this way.

Cassandra wanted to hear about Mr. Middleton. She believed her parents to be sealing up a deal with a Mr. Crowley from the neighboring town. I recounted Mr. Middleton's afternoon visit to sate her interest and swore them to secrecy. They didn't seem particularly impressed or unnerved. I yearned for either response, to anchor my own.

"Well, is he cute?" Cassandra asked, twirling a dishwater blonde lock.

I didn't know how to answer her. Unlike Stacie and me, Cassandra had always liked boys—but husbands were not like boys. I didn't know how to make her understand what it was really like, but I also had the feeling that Cassandra would handle things much differently when it was her turn. I was thankful when Stacie changed the subject to school, with stories of pencils stolen from the teacher's desk and guest story-readers, even though they made me both wistful and angry, and Stacie knew it.

THE NIGHT BEFORE THE CEREMONY, my parents entertained their friends with chilled rosé wine and a CD of lulling smooth jazz on repeat. My mother dusted my cheekbones with her dark blush and checked my back to make sure I wore a trainer. I was to greet guests at the door until everyone had arrived, and then Stacie and I could retreat to the basement to play Barbies together one last time. According to tradition, Mr. Middleton was not invited; it was to be his last bachelor night alone. But Mr. Woodward and Esmerelda came, and Mr. Silverstein, and Stacie's and Cassandra's parents, eager to know how it had all been pulled off. Mr. Baker said, as if surprised, "You look very pretty tonight, Mary Ellen," and then he and Mr. Weir stood together in the corner, shaking their heads. The Calderóns arrived last. Mr. Calderón was so old his eyes constantly watered, and he could barely speak or hear anything. Mrs. Calderón was a young grandmother, her braided hair still long and black. She bent to me and whispered, "You're not getting cold feet now, are you, dear?"

"Cold feet?" I asked. I peered down at my slipper socks, embarrassed I'd removed the Mary Janes.

"I tried to run away from this one." She winked at her husband, but his expression didn't change. "But then, I always misbehaved."

Mr. Calderón held tight to her arm, and she guided him patiently toward the drinks. She kissed his shaking hand, then placed in it a glass of water.

In the basement, adult feet shifting above us, I understood that Mrs. Calderón had been saying that she knew me and that she understood. From tomorrow on, that would be me upstairs, like Esmerelda and even my mother, laughing a stupid laugh and making frequent trips to the bathroom, with an eye on my husband and his eye on me. Mrs. Calderón had issued me a playful dare and made no promises; but if it was the last childlike thing I did, I would take her up on it.

"Stacie, I need your help."

She stopped pushing her Barbie car, a convertible she'd

acquired from me in a trade, and said with suspicion, "You do?"

As I explained what I wanted to do, Stacie's eyes began to gleam. At one point she took my hand. I felt close to her, until she said, "You won't be married first after all!" But still she was my confidante, my partner with her own stake.

What we came up with wasn't much of a plan, but we did identify the basic elements required in running away: a note, a lightly packed suitcase, and utter secrecy. My mother had already packed most of my clothes into a luggage set embroidered with my new initials, M.M. I removed the lightest bag from the pile by the side door and had Stacie sneak it back home with her. After slipping away, having deposited the note in a spot both clandestine and sure to be eventually discovered, I would call Stacie from a pay phone and have her meet me with the suitcase. For this purpose, I used my new skills to sew a quarter into the hem of my dress, which hung, long and white, like a ghost, outside my closet door.

Beneath the covers with a flashlight that night, I composed the note to Mr. Middleton. I could not tell him, as they did in fantasy romance movies, that I had met someone else. What I wrote was this:

Dear Mr. Middleton,

I am sorry to leave you at the alter. You seem very nice but I can not be a wife. Please do not try to find me and please try to go on with your life.

Mary Ellen

I thought it sounded quite grown-up and made running away on cold feet seem a serious and viable act. I wasn't worried that we hadn't decided where I would go. I didn't consider then that I knew of no woman who was not a wife, that anyone I might turn to would turn me in, that breach of contract was serious business and punishable by law. I believed two things: that getting away would be the hardest part of the game, and that you could only plan as far as you could see. I don't know if I believed that I would make it, but I believed that I would try.

I might have left that very night, cutting Stacie's ties to my venture, but I had a romantic notion of wearing that dress. I pictured kicking off the white patent-leather shoes to run faster and the small train flailing behind me. I pictured that the dress would dirty as I ran, it would rip and tear, and then I would know I was free.

WHEN WE ARRIVED AT THE CHAPEL, I spied Mr. Middleton's car in the parking lot. During a covert trip to the "potty," I slipped the note beneath its windshield wipers. It had always made me laugh that my parents never noticed an advertisement attached in this way until they were driving.

In the bride's room, Dad, his eyes shiny and red-rimmed, was smoothing out the fold from the contract, to which my signature was to be added. "Why don't you go sit down, Frank?" my mother suggested, but she stayed with me, adjusting my dress and hairspraying my hot-roller curls, until the final moments. She hovered in the doorway. "You are wearing, aren't you, all the things we talked about? You remember how it goes? Something old, something new, something borrowed, something blue, and a silver sixpence for your shoe?"

"I remembered," I said, thinking of the sewn quarter. If I wasn't careful to keep my skirt held as I walked, the coin would hit the floor with the barest knock. "Mommy, can I have a few minutes alone? This is a very big day for me."

She looked surprised, but her face softened. "Boy, kid, you really have grown up." She kissed my cheek, then rubbed it furiously to remove any trace of lipstick. I felt sad, at that moment, to think that I would never see her again, and wondered if she would privately count me lucky or only be disappointed.

The air outside smelled like a fall barbecue, charring corn and sausages. In the bright blue sky flew a V of birds. Just as I took a breath to run, I spotted Mr. Middleton across the lot next to his car. The collar of his tuxedo was misaligned; he had skipped a buttonhole and set the whole thing off. Facing the sun, he held one hand to his face—to shield his eyes?—and in the other was my note. His shoulders seemed to be shaking with laughter. Had he been about to run away himself when he came upon my note? This possibility, however remote, might have been what led me to walk straight toward him, slowly, steadily, wholly of my own volition. I hate to believe, especially now, that it was as simple as holding to my nature; that I was just a good girl who did always as she was told, without hope and without design.

"Mary Ellen?" he said. "You're still here." I saw as I came closer that he'd actually been crying, not laughing; a tear dropped from the left-side curl of his moustache. I thought of something Dad often said, when, much younger, I'd get caught up in venturesome play with inevitable consequences: "It's all fun and games, isn't it, until someone gets hurt?"

"I'm still here," I said. I raised my arms to indicate I should be lifted and let Mr. Middleton cradle me against his chest. I felt his wildly beating heart, and he began to stroke my hair as if I needed calming down. But my stomach felt only the faintest rumble of hunger, an emptiness. I knew that I had done the right thing, the only thing I could, but still, I felt foolish. If I were really as smart as everyone believed, I would never have found myself in this situation, with a ridiculous man I was obligated to care for. My escape would have been better planned and better executed. He would never have taken an interest in the first place.

"Mary," he said, "you do know that I—"

"What?" I struggled to sit up in his arms, impatient suddenly, and restless. I wanted to go inside, where everyone was waiting, and get it over with.

He set me down on the hood of his car and began again. "I think you'll be very pleased with the life I want to give you."

I stared through his windshield at the tan leather seats, sculpted to hug a body as the vehicle took the curves. I saw where the top would fold down. This car would take me to my new home.

"You do understand, don't you, that the deal is irrevo-cable? If you were to run off, your parents would owe me a great deal of money. They could never hope to come out of debt."

I knew that was a threat, and thought lowly of him for it. But then he said something I look back on now as the beginning of my new understanding of my life. "I'm yours, Mary Ellen, and if you stay, all that is mine will be yours too."

In answer, I rebuttoned his shirt.

AS I SIGNED THE CONTRACT, my eyes slid down the page, its tiny print in a formal, inscrutable language. The sum my parents had provided to Mr. Middleton seemed enormous, though I know it now to be less than the cost of my childhood home and much less than the worth of Mr. Middleton's company. Men who'd planned poorly would seek a much larger dowry and might suffer for it in their choice of wives. It was our parents, always looking toward the future, who put money first. The dowry, like a child that would grow, was ultimately an investment.

I handed over the paper for the minister to stamp, and he pronounced us man and wife.

MR. MIDDLETON HAS KEPT MY NOTE folded in his sock drawer, and for years he has teased me for having misspelled "altar." Putting away his clean laundry, I look at it sometimes, not with wistfulness or shame, but because I want to remember. The contract itself is in a safety deposit box; I'll receive a key for my eighteenth birthday, a day now close in sight. The Barbies, of course, are long gone. Dad succeeded in overriding my mother, and the toys stayed in the basement a year into my marriage. But I rarely played with them—they seemed to have lost their allure, and I never knew what they wanted to do or say or wear. Stacie still hadn't been promised, and I offered them to her, but she pretended not to be interested. She and Cassandra were thick as thieves then. "Save them for your kids," she said, and we couldn't help but dissolve into panicked laughter. By the time she was taken, at age fourteen, she was serious about having children. It is her husband who insists they wait. If we see each other now at the supermarket, grocery baskets in hand, we merely nod in greeting. We have so little in common.

Mr. Middleton has made me apprentice to his business, which he says one day, when he is dead, I will take over. Even if—and the decision to have children is entirely up to me, he says—we have a son. This is highly unusual and very progressive, Dad has told me. He patted my head and told me he was proud. I looked for something like greed or jealousy in his eyes, but found only love. My mother admitted, over afternoon tea, that she wishes Dad had done something similar for her. As far as I can see, he long ago reached his height on the ladder. What could he have done for her?

"I have good business sense, a ruthless mind," she insisted, and gestured to the piles of butterscotch-chip scones she'd baked for a block sale. "But I suppose I'm lucky, in that we fell in love."

I nodded in agreement, though I knew what would provoke her: *But isn't it easier if we don't think of love?* Visiting is difficult because, although they think they act differently, my parents still treat me like a child, a newlywed bride. They don't recognize what I've become, but they won't argue when the time comes to face it, when Dad retires and I, with Mr. Middleton's money, am in charge of them. Their investment in me will have its rewards. I want the best for them, as they've managed for me.

After a morning spent at home with my private tutor, Ms. Dundee—whose husband succumbed when she was much younger and much prettier (she says) to a condition she won't speak of—I change into a navy skirt and Peter Pan–collar blouse, hop on my bike, and head in to the office. Mr. Middleton has given me a fine car, of course, but I normally prefer the exercise. So far I just prepare after-lunch coffee and bring it in on a tray, each cup made to the preference of each board member. Mr. Middleton sits at the head of the table. His moustache, after all these years, remains; he would shave it if I asked, but I suspect that issuing that demand would expose me somehow. Once situated beside him, I'm encouraged to listen in and, if so inclined, take notes. But it's the quiet power struggle that interests me, the way his inferiors look at him and how they cover their desires with neutral jargon, loyal reports. He takes for granted, I think, the way things are now.

"You've learned a lot so far from just watching and listening," he says to me, winking, as I take out my pad of paper. I turn away and roll my eyes: he believes we're always in on some joke. This one is meant to be in reference to the nights I join him in his bedroom, on the floor above mine. Mostly I just lie there while he touches my hair or my back, as he once demonstrated with the doll. He has mentioned, in those moments, love and a feeling of fulfillment. For him they may be the same thing. Yet even with me around, taking care of things, I sense he's still a lonely man. I feel guilty sometimes, offering so little reimbursement for his attentions, though he receives more pleasure from them than I do, and I've made attempts to do for him what other girls and young wives have described. Now I believe that the hardest part of the game is staying in it, holding on to your stake. And that you can't plan too far into the future. I've taken this down in my notes: *The benefits mature with time*. I've begun to appreciate just how much work parents invest in their children, and wives in their husbands; it's only fair for the investor to become a beneficiary.

BLOODFEUD
\\\\\\\

THE EYE IS IN THE PEEPHOLE AGAIN, watching me
through the picket fence. Mother's told me not to speak
a word, not *Go away, skank*, or *Bitch, I know you're there*,
or even *Good day, how do you do?* and never, ever to let
her in the backyard or infiltrate her own—to, in sum,
stop fucking with her. Fences make good neighbors, the
women like to say, and before Bill Conley killed him, Father built ours tall, taller even than himself, so it couldn't
be climbed, and without space between the slats. Mother
says it needs repainting, but she has got too much other
shit to do. For me, it's always been this dingy white; I
don't recall when it was standing sparkling new, although

the days that Father labored, hammering boards he let me think my strength alone held in place, are still fresh in my mind. The first insults between our families had just been flung, and it'd been so long since I'd seen Father out of his chair, his face so full of sweat and blood.

I'm the one who put it there. The hole. It's big enough to put a finger through, but you'd be stupid to do that. I'm surprised the skank trusts her eyeball in it, and on a day so crisp I can see her eyelid dip to blink, so close to fall's first game, I'm set on acing perfect stunts.

I fake a start for another handspring across the lawn, running instead straight for the fence until my palms slam up against it. She doesn't step off or get scared, just keeps looking on all cryptic and calm, like a fish you're not sure can even see you outside its tank, much less comprehend a coexisting realm of creatures walking and breathing air. I stand blinking my eye right next to hers. The color's not the plain honey-brown it seems from far away; instead her iris has got little flecks of violet and gold in it, just like her dear old dad, Mr. Conley—or so I start to imagine; I'd never seen the man up close—which makes me want to punch it in, but Mother's come out from the kitchen.

"The fuck you doing, Izzy? I thought you came out here to play."

"Play? I *was* practicing." Some mothers understand the importance of these drills, while other mothers are the why of cheer squad getting no respect. I only get so much time to myself after school before she has me hanging wash, scrubbing potatoes. It isn't easy to pull a decent cartwheel or split when a mole's got sights on you.

It's nothing like going up before a crowd under the lights. "What am I supposed to do? Pretend she doesn't stare like a horny lesbian?"

Mother folds her muscled forearms across her flour-dusted chest, the frown on her face sending wrinkles to her brow. I bet her whole scalp beneath her tightly bunned hair is taut from all the shifting skin it takes to express her inner state. She's always quick to defend the women who've taken up in pairs at one house, raising children or not, talking into the night, cuddled for warmth; or at least she claims to believe what goes on in anyone's bedroom is no other body's business. "Do I open your door to catch you masturbating or talk about it with my friends?" she'll say to prove her point. I don't touch myself, not ever—who would I think about, when most of the boys left around are younger than Ernie or not much older—but she knows the accusation shuts me up.

"That's what I told you, is it not?" she says now. "Ignore the damn fool. Come on and help your brother; there's work for you to do."

The screen bangs shut on her behind. I don't follow, not right away. The football that Ernie left in the middle of the yard is lying laces up where I kicked it from my way. Him playing the momma's boy is what gets me called out. I punt it high above the fence and listen to the Conley girl's feet run and the cushioned rustling as it lands, likely in a row of her mother's greens. After a beat, the ball sails weakly back, wobbling longways, side-to-side, like its torpedo shape was built with resistance instead of speed and torque in mind. I catch it, then hurl it at the ground for a touchdown dance. I'm gone before I have to see if the eye is back.

IF I ONLY HAD TO DEAL WITH the skank next door at home, that'd be one thing. The fence is between us, so while I nearly smell her breath, I never have to see her face. But even on the schoolyard, she's watching me.

Atop the monkey bars, all by herself, she scrawls pencil to paper and meets my eyes. I'm lined up with my girls by the graffitied brick, drilling cheers for Friday's game. Conley's the only one who picked the school uniform with culotte shorts; one suspender hangs unhooked, clinking the metal bar, while ours swish in double loops against our skirts. Pathetic. At the fore, Jill's screaming out some basic rah-rah sis-boom-bah. We bend over, stick out our butts, and shake our racks. The wind blows through our hair and travels on, trapping leaves and plastic bags against the legs of the swings, released to be caught again at the jungle gym. The seats left behind are empty, swinging ghosts.

We've got a pyramid half built—no girl yet on my back—when a lower, coed grade files out from the school, signaling our recess is done. Teacher's blowing her whistle. Still we linger in our pose. What would be hidden by helmets and padding on the field make a strange sight to see: crewcuts mingled with pig- and ponytails, the subtle differences in their prepubescent shapes. The boys pinch the girls and pull on their hair; the girls stand straight, modeling good behavior. Mother says we'll see if this time they can learn or if it's nature.

We break the pyramid for a line, and I fall in with Jill. Squad leader has to be skinny, it's like a rule; this one has the kind of skinny you just know is in her blood, not to be matched—even if, like her, you chewed just gum for lunch, stretching it pink from mouth to finger. Nerve of that Conley bitch: out of nowhere, cutting between, she slides a hand over my pocket, tucks in a folded square of paper. "Meet me by the fence," she says hot and muddled to my ear. "It's about our dads."

At first I'm too appalled to reply. I burst, "Fuck you have to say about my dad?"

Jill turns with eyes of ice. Conley steps back to retreat, but my girls gather and descend, confining Conley to a circle. Her gaze is on the ground, curtained by limp strands of hair. Teacher's striding toward us, whistle shining wet pulled from her lips. "Now, now, girls," she's saying.

I set a hand on the bone of Conley's shoulder, give it a shove. Then her limp strands are in my fist, I get an elbow to her chest. My girls start to chant, *go, go, fight, fight.* They circle us like planets. The bigger ones, the ones who form the base of the pyramid with me, crowd in to try and pry us apart. I shove on for the blacktop and take her with me. Up close she stinks of outside air, not perfume or soap. I call her every name I can think: *cunt, motherfucker, whore.* She is silent, throat blooming patches of red as I throttle the breath from it.

"That's enough, Isabelle!" Teacher cries, pushing through. "You'll kill her!" But I only stop because she won't fight back. Because it's probably what she wanted, she enjoyed it.

Later, alone, outside the principal's, I pull her note out

from my pocket. *Peephole @ midnight. I'm not my dad, and yours wasn't the perfect man you think. They're passed, and we're just us. Can't a Fischer and a Conley come out together on the other side?*

THERE'S BEEN NO CAUSE TO PUNISH a fight in some time, but what's settled on for me is one week's suspension from class, counting extracurriculars. When I call the principal a shriveled-up old marm who never even had a man around to defend her family's honor and kill or get killed, she makes it two—but if I can't be at Friday's game, it hardly matters.

At home, Mother knows better than to speak of it. The afternoon's no different than any other: I scrub, Mother peels. She's disappointed, embarrassed, probably pissed, but I bet even more she's glad I'll be around more to help. Meanwhile Ernie's got a friend out back, tossing the pigskin. Eleven years old, and along with a handful of other boys, they made varsity. Now I can't even watch him play, much less cheer him on. My brother's not one of the biggest on the field, not like his flabby friend, but I taught him to play to his advantage, ran him ragged through the cones same way Coach did to me, ran him worse. I've seen the new lineup at practice: he's one of the fastest, darting through holes that close up before anyone's noticed. His skinny little arms are starting to take on the shape of muscle, his chest to square and widen out. One day he's going to wake up a man, and what kind, he can only credit to Mother or me. I'm just glad he wasn't older, when it happened.

He waves the boy to stand back for his throw, and I wonder if he knows, if he's showing off for her. If there's one thing I hate more than that skank watching me, it's the thought of her eyes on Ernie.

"Who is that fat punk, anyway? You think it's such a great idea that Ernie hangs with him? Who's his people?"

Absently, Mother recites what may as well be the motto of the truce but which I know makes up her own guiding philosophy. "Diplomacy breeds peace."

"Or does reaching out just get your hand cut off?"

Steady, Mother mans the knife.

"What was Mr. Conley like?"

She keeps peeling, slipping the skin in a spiral. "Let the dead rest, Isabelle."

"Was he a jerk? Tell lewd jokes? Drink too much?"

"Just what kind of shit you trying to stir?" She studies me over the blade; the peel breaks. I look down at a potato tossing between my hands. *Couch potato*, she called Father, when she was feeling sympathetic of his plight, which wasn't often. I let the potato rest. She takes it and sighs. "It wasn't personal, you know that, Izzy. A stupid bar fight turned deadly started it all. Revenge goaded those feuds on, a mania to put wrong back to right. All over, what, a couple dollars owed, a saved pool table stolen—and don't you listen to talk, no woman was at fault, that first killing or ever. Each man did it to his own sorry self."

"I know all that. I mean, how was he as a person, otherwise."

"He was a hard worker when the plant was up, a family man, just like your father." She speaks fierce, then wistful. "Like most. They never did stop thinking of us. Too proud."

I don't want to hear that crock about how Bill Conley's sucker shot was out of love, loyalty, pride. I want to know the whole truth, his weaknesses, shames, mistakes.

"Was he pathetic like her?" I press. "A little weird, have no friends?"

She stares at me hard, pointing the knife. "I think missing your daddy, having no uncles or grandpa left alive, could make a little girl turn out weird. You ever thought about that?"

I scrub another clump of mud from a potato dug up fresh from our ground. I'm not dense, and Mother's hardly subtle.

"I'm not like that," I say. "I'm not like her."

THAT NIGHT PEERING FROM MY WINDOW at shadows cast over the stretch of lawn that we use to play, the turned earth that we use to grow, I think about the ways the men died over the years. A bullet, a knife, an IED: killing was easy enough, given the proper tool and surrender or surprise. Geralds did it to Evans with his own bare hands, after the man poisoned his cousin via his drink. I think about the night Father stayed late at the bar, how Mrs. Conley came to the door and Mother fell at her feet. Ernie just stood there with his thumb stuck in his mouth, watching that woman hold our mother while both of them wept. I sent him to his room, and when he tried to come out, crying and scared, I blocked the door. It was to protect him, toughen him up.

I shot that hole through the fence, sorry it wasn't a man. The day the new rosters were hung, I dug up the gun, the bullet Mother had buried beside it like a seed, too distraught to know I watched. Just like Father, in the bar—after all, he'd fired fine once before that night, taking out his feckless former foreman—I'd had my chance to stop the cycle short, and I'd blown it, shooting blind. Father, scoping Conley slinking in through the back, still sporting black for his feckless brother, must have known what would come next. If he had only been first on the trigger, sure in his aim, there would have been no more Conleys, no male left to come back on him. I never said to that girl or anyone that Father was a perfect man.

I know what she, that Conley girl, thinks, brainwashed by the truce. That her note has me on the edge of remorse, recalling how mine struck first when her uncle, the foreman, fell—a man not a father, but a husband, a son, a brother. That the fight, her easy defeat, letting me win without struggle, could turn us friends, practically blood sisters. I make her wait in the dark. I never come.

FAR OFF, THE STADIUM ALIGHT looks like a landed ship, and closer up, the women solo or in pairs, straining to fill the stands, look waiting to be brought into another world—patient and calm, not cheering at all. At halftime, the scoreboard shows a tie. I've missed coed JV, who opened up; this is varsity, more male than ever. We split our teams in two to play against ourselves, in ever-shifting divisions, a trick of the truce to emphasize we are all on the same side. Other towns have nothing to do with us.

I spy gray-haired Mrs. Conley in the crowd next to Mother, raw work-hands at fidgety rest in their laps, and I duck quick beneath the bleachers. She must have already promised it won't happen again, the first time is the last, apologized on my behalf. Puberty, she blames it on, or my getting bumped for more boys from football to cheer. I told her, I'm over it. I know with whom I belong. Conley sits alone toward the front, just like in class to suck up. I recognize her from below by her clean saddle shoes, not inked and signed like everyone else's, and snake nearer through the metal bars crisscrossing hard lines in the shadows. Above, and all around, stadium lights shine piercing bright, but less like day than like a circle of stationary moons. The announcer's voice echoes shrilly, followed by lackluster claps, and through the slats I glimpse the squad rushing the field for the show. I like the way our legs look moving together, smooth and shiny and bare, scissoring in splits and kicks. *Our* because even though I'm not up there with my girls, I'm still a part. My mind's in sync with the routine, whether or not they feel my watch.

And it must be they can't. In the pyramid, Jill has to take my place at the base, and I can see she's shaky; she can't take the weight. She would, if she knew I was watching, if only to prove a point—that she's as strong as me. As the formation buckles, collapsing apart, I'm filled with a weird swell: of glee, or of pride. This is why I don't at first notice the pristine shoes lifting up and stepping off the stands. By the time I zero in, Conley's made it to where Ernie's in a huddle with his boys. She's at his back, laying a hand on his bicep, just a weak spindly stick as compared to his padded-up shoulders. He turns, and I'm on the move even before her lips part and tip down toward his ear.

I have a right to hear what she'll say, though I already have a good idea of what that is. That our father was less than a man in facing death, that he begged for life—cited us, me and Ernie, his bright and shining lights in a world turned dark, every circuit on the grid with one switch. She might not go so far in her lies, but he really did call us that. I can't have her talking shit to Ernie. He's too young to take it; she'll rattle his return to the field. Football is all boys have.

I break from the bleachers and feel Mother rising behind, a great frown stretching her face. Outside the huddle, femme as Coach is dyke, Teacher lowers her clipboard to nudge the principal. The old marm calls out. Conley sees me coming but doesn't quit. My brother's cheeks go pale to rose as she speaks, eyes on me, her eyes always on me, and yet I slow because I get his blush isn't for sadness or rage. His teammates are all laughter and jeers. He *likes* that she has come to him, has no regard for the past, for age or blood, for what people will say. She flips the limp strands of her hair and flashes teeth like she's the same as me or Jill, but she is not: she meets his puppy-dog gaze in her usual unflinching lonely way, failing to get that her slouching back and fading smile give her fake confidence away. What has she whispered, *I'm rooting for you, I hope you win?* Like it's just Ernie alone against everyone on the field.

I shouldn't be surprised at what stunt she plays next, and I know it's only meant to get me back, rile me up, but still it stops me in my tracks.

Conley leans in to kiss the side of his lips, like he's a boy who belongs to her and no one's son or brother. The stadium seems to hush, and my girls drop their fists punched out in V's, slow, one by one. It's something nobody's seen in a long while.

OLD MAID
\\\\\\\

I'D LIVED NOT THREE YEARS in the house at the top of the hill at the end of the street when I learned that I'd been anointed the old maid. As in, *Lights were on late up at the old maid's. Think she had company?* (Insert chuckles.) And, *Why not have the old maid to dinner—not much fun at these things in round numbers.* And, *Let's go out like we used to. The old maid will watch the kids. They love she actually reads them every page.*

Some of these people I'd called my friends, though I had nicknames for them too: the Cleavers and the Huxtables, just with the races reversed. When they were young and I was new, we'd gotten falling-down drunk, knee-deep in liquor cabinets, up to our elbows in wine cellars. While their children, babies really, slept overdosed on warm milk, we rolled up the rugs to dance. Ward made passes at me in the hallway, my coat heaped beneath the others on the bed; Clair clung to my arm in the kitchen and made confessions. I'd showered them with gifts when they became again expectant, and to their kids, older now and full of questions, tried to explain: When a man and a woman—no. Mommies have a kind of soil, and Daddies a kind of seed. The big white bird brings the pouch clamped in his beak.

They listened to everything. It was the little Huxtables who finked.

"Finking isn't nice," I said. ". . . Mommy really calls me that?"

They nodded, curls bouncing gold about their necks. I tucked the sheets in to their chins, dimpled like Daddy's. The pout in the girl's lips, the chub in the boy's cheeks— these would thin with time. The baby sleeping in the next room already usurped them in softness.

"Is it bad?" asked little Theo.

That's when I thought to toss the book aside, or at least start skipping pages.

That evening on, I enjoyed sending their children off to dreamland's shifting currents cradled in a nest of my own bedtime tales. The stories slipped from my tongue as though culled from the air as my fingers combed the tangles from their curls. The only hungering a child can comprehend is the ache of an empty stomach: I built up a hut of candy and carved out a burning hearth. Consumption, consummation: there is a point in being lost where no devouring can satisfy. In my renditions, the old maid baked and ate the kids.

Their eyes grew wide and then clenched shut, and finally they'd drift from me, anchored by their little bodies to their beds, and wake back with their parents, where they belonged. The fairy castles would dissolve, but whatever shadows they'd collected in the night they'd carry with them. This was part of growing up.

They weren't mine, but I did love them, all of them.

After the Huxtables came home on that first night, Cliff and I shared a nightcap by the fire, Clair too tired. You wouldn't know it if you asked of his day at work—grave toward his profession, respectful of his patients' ills—but he was the extrovert, she the one so often curled inside. He was giddy from the game, an unexpected home-team win, cracking jokes in reenactments; I laughed, feeling the effects of whiskey splashed with water and nothing else. He was a purer Cliff than Cosby ever was, but he did wave from the window, watching my hips swinging me home.

The subtle rise of the street was such that you only stumbled if uncertain of the ground beneath. The hill at the end was sudden and steep, but the house that sat on top was not a prize to pin your hopes to, no crown for having joined and won the rat race. A single story planed horizontal, it must've looked modern once, striking in its minimalism when it was built, but it wasn't grand enough to reign above the others, stacked tall and archaically ornate to make up for their lesser view. For all its soaring floor-to-ceiling glass, it seemed to lay low in the trees, stretching only with the roofline, long and flat. A set of stairs took you up, handrailed and carved into the hillside. These wound right past my windowed walls into the wooded peak, a public park from which to see the bay and lights from the city. Even in the dark, without dimension, you could sense the wetness of the water from the sky. You had visions of leaping off to fly above, the cotton wisps of the clouds' quick-licking vapors.

You'd think no one could blame my curtains being closed, night and day. Even with the strips of shiny tape, birds crashed, breaking their necks. Death shouldn't turn into a chore, the sweeping up, the constant digging of graves. Early or late, some neighbor from another street was always bobbing by, their dog off leash. I blamed no one who'd looked in: a house that hovered over, exposed. They'd seen my table with the one chair scooted out and three pushed in, my bed unmade in half. My books that lined the walls, my upright piano. I kept it neat but didn't dust—cobwebs another pleasure housewives wouldn't understand.

I never saw myself growing old, alone or otherwise. True, I was the only one among my grade-school friends who hadn't cared to conjure up a white dress and veil. In high school I was too busy, fooling around; college likewise no place for a boyfriend. As an adult, at work, I never spoke of a partner, but I had lived off and on with a man for five years, and another for seven, with three years in between. I'd stopped referring to the first by any name at all; the second, because both his names began the same, I called simply "A."

Spending an inheritance in one shot is nothing like letting loose a bird from its cage—even if the sum is so surprising it seems to nearly touch your grief. When it came, A was gone and hadn't deigned to send a card, yet even without him, I still felt that pull, after years of renting one-rooms, for something permanent. My bid on the house was low for the neighborhood, but the seller, the middle-aged married son, wanted a buyer who wouldn't tear it down. In assisted living, his dad still spoke of future generations; the grandfather had built it. I'd told the son—childless, and older than me—that I'd be crazy not to stay here for the rest of my life. Privately, I thought that this was where I'd probably die, excruciatingly sane.

I took out all my books from storage, and my sister agreed, with all this space, that the piano neither of us had much played should go to me. I wallpapered the walls a decadent gilded brocade I knew would never make it past a man; it'd have to be grandfathered in. I was young enough I thought that there would be at least one more, but after that last, felt I deserved another break. The only men I saw those days, apart from those at work and on the long commute—so long I rarely stayed late anymore in the city—were the husbands on my street, and no matter what they might've thought, I didn't want them. Ward just liked to see me blush, and Cliff to hear me laugh. They both wanted to believe that one of us wouldn't be so easily cowed by the fondness and respect we each held for their wives.

The old maid. A solitary woman stayed young only by living wickedly. I'd been to them a disappointment.

It didn't even take a month of telling stories. June called one Saturday and said her boys were having nightmares. Wally wouldn't admit it, but he whimpered and tossed and turned and was wetting the bed, and Beaver woke them all in tears. They'd been telling tall tales to their friend Eddie down the block, and the recurring motif was that I was a witch who lusted after children's flesh. She had wanted to see if I was free that night to babysit, but now she wasn't sure. She waited for me to speak.

"Well, if they're so afraid of me, maybe it's not a good idea. I hope that doesn't spoil your plans last minute. I was thinking anyway of seeing friends in the city."

She put a smile in her voice. "You do that, honey." As though we weren't the same age, as though she could've birthed me.

Something scratched then at the window, a rustling of leaves. I peeled the curtain back to see their little legs running, their little fingers clutching sticks trussed into crosses. I made a point of never turning on the lights that night, not until after twelve, and not for long.

Later that week I brought a cat home from a shelter, and within days had her known as my familiar.

Clair climbed the steps one evening, jaunty in her jogging clothes. She plucked one earbud from her ear, let it drop, smoothed an errant frizzy strand inside her ponytail, rapped on the door. Usually she only made confessions after a drink, so I poured her one. We took our glasses into the trees. The sun would be setting, dusk already in the canopy.

"I'd love another," she assured me once she'd made

her revelation, "but Christ, I only just had Nessa. I can't believe it's even possible. We've made love, what, twice since?"

"Three already seems a crowd," I remarked. "What does Cliff say to a fourth?"

"I don't know if I want to tell him." Clair looked at me with eyes that seemed a little wild, dilating with the loss of light. "Have you ever . . . ? I mean, I don't know enough about your . . . past situations, if you would have wanted—if you would regret—"

"If, seeing where I am now, I regret it?" I finished for her. None of them had ever asked why I was single, if they could set me up, not that I'd let them. I must've been the only young attractive unattached person they knew. I let her imagination unfurl: I'd had an abortion, three, and now was barren; I'd given one away at sixteen, then tried to steal him back at thirty-three; he didn't want me.

She looked over quizzically. "Your house has been so dark on weekends I just assumed, and June too, that you had someone in the city. We're always staring up wistfully."

That wasn't true. They were smug about their fates next to mine.

"So you have your nights of fun," she said. "You deserve it after the week."

Then that was it, the fear, the fantasy, what she saw for herself in my place: I was off on one-night stands. Clair took my arm, nearly tripping on the path, tinkling ice in her glass. We'd emerged into the clearing, heading for where the side dropped off in a dizzy tumbling of rocks.

The sun was slipping down between buildings in the city, and brake lights lined the bridge in red, headlights in white; water shimmering in a million ever-changing crests and troughs.

"I miss *work*," she said. "My job wasn't so great, not what I wanted to do, but at least then I was more free."

I started to laugh, and so did she, remembering, maybe, the early stages of careers: cages of cubicles, timed fifteen-minute breaks. After jobs in many different offices, mine *was* what I wanted, or the closest I might come. I had walls and a window, and I didn't want to stop for water-cooler chats. But it did not make me feel free.

"*Adventure*," she said. "The possibility. Knowing no one would have to know where I was going, what I had done."

"I hope I don't have to say it," I said, "but you can trust me. Any kind of help you need."

I did mean it. Without looking over, she squeezed my arm. Once Clair let you in, she really was very warm. We sat in the grass and cheersed, and it was only then I noticed that, while my glass had been half-emptied, hers she hadn't even been sipping. The old maid, all the while, had been sharing in the confidence of a mother.

Not a month after that, their house went up, Cliff driving down the sign himself.

"They need a bigger place, you know," June said when I passed her on the street. She wore an apron, an actual apron, and actual high-heeled shoes going out to get the mail. Her hair was a fantastic gathered mess of little plaits. Ward's car turned the corner; he was late. We once discussed a carpool, but I'd have had to take a bus and train to meet him closer by the bridge. I'd wanted to tell June "I do know," or with my special knowledge could've foreseen, but felt jilted, somehow, seeing him at the ends of our separate commutes. Climbing the stairs, the strap of the laptop I'd been lugging—over the ferry, through the hills—cut hard into my shoulder.

One Saturday night, I heard the voices of sprites and stepped barefoot outside. Those and the stars led me deep into the trees. My house behind was good as gone, the lights all out, but inside I really did have company: some man I'd picked up from the ferry. I'd told him not to come until the sun had set; now he was sleeping. Ahead on the path, the flash of a pair of eyes: only my cat, out stalking shadows and mice. She bounded away from me into the brush. Each step, the rough uncovered earth ground against my uncallused feet.

I found them dancing on the clearing, flashing handheld lights. When they saw me, they circled in, flitting like bugs. They grasped me by the legs, and I kissed them each atop their golden curls. Then prancing off they went again. Cliff was standing so close to the drop the slightest nudge could've sent him tumbling. He'd turned at his children's cries but didn't as I came beside him.

"The witching hour," he joked, gesturing to the sky. It wasn't really very late. "Trying to get them unafraid of the dark."

"Seen any?" I asked. We looked down, not out at the lights, close enough to touch had touching been what we wanted. The scent of that man in my bed was rising off of me, a heat in the cool air. If there was a moment, it was in the abyss, more about the pull of nothingness than sex, exactly. Between us seemed the recognition that to slip would have meant fulfillment of a longing, not for a climactic end, but to enter into fathomless mystery.

"Mommy!" the children cried. It would have been a preternatural sight to see: Clair in a twirl with her cherubs, girl and boy, wearing white. Clair rosy from her exertion up the stairs, an infant strapped to her back and her belly round and full as the moon. But a little one must have tripped and had a spill: there was a shriek and a silence of gathering strength. The weeping rolled out slow and steady, building to a howl that broke back to child from animal.

Cliff and I stepped apart with unthinking smiles as they encroached. Clair was towing the girl by the hand, the boy sniveling at her side—no place for him anymore to be taken up, her body balanced by dual weights, back and front. Sweat ran from her temples, her mane fluffed out loose and lioness. The infant kicked out her legs and cooed, happy enough.

"What are you two so smug about?" Clair said.

Within a week I learned their house had sold to newlyweds. The two couples in the process had hit it off, so the Cleavers were having a party: farewell to the Huxtables, welcome home to the A——s.

The A——s. It couldn't be.

But it was. I recognized A by his back, broad but gently sloped, in a dress shirt, not a flannel. He poured a drink at the counter, and when he spun to hand it off—

to a bottle-blonde, much younger woman, ring clinking the glass—our eyes glanced. You never would've known the jolt that passed us through, all the careful rearranging we had to do on the inside. I tried to picture what he'd glimpsed. My former self, the one a decade back he had first met, superimposed on the present: gloss-black hair and a wry smile. Surely not my strands of gray, not my crow's feet, not from across the room. These new features had been creeping up on me over the years. Now that I was known as the old maid, they stood out.

We shook hands when introduced. His hair had thinned, and he must've been wearing lenses, for both his eyes were brown, instead of one half green. I don't know how the pretending came so easy, for me. For him, it was for her. I could see what he had seen. Pert features, porcelain skin, a body same as it was at thirteen. She was deadly serious, for being so young, but when he teased her, seldom and gently, she giggled. Her clothes, cut simply, had the sheen of quality. They could not have been purchased by him, unless his vocation along with his character had been changed.

I kept close to Clair and Cliff, on the premise I'd miss them so. Clair kept one hand on her belly, one on Cliff's knee, and he teased us as he never would were she alone with him. "Will you still call each other to plan your outfits out?" We both had on filmy scarves and metallic-colored shoes. Ward eyed us from an armchair, scrolling the screen of his phone, until June beckoned that the A——s wanted a tour of his collection: R&B records, jazz, gospel, and soul. Nobody danced, and we never made it past champagne. It was not until the bedroom, fetching my coat, that A and I spoke more than pleasantries.

"From what they told me," he said from behind, "I had no idea it would be you."

"Could say the same," I said, still pawing the pile through. My coat had started at the top and somehow sunk to the bottom. "I never pictured an 's' put on your name."

"You do know why they have to hold you at arm's length?" He was right at my neck. For seven years he'd had me in the habit of pinning up my hair; now it was down. The rest he said to my ear: "The men want to fuck you, and the women want to be you, being fucked by their husbands."

It was the kind of propaganda a husband knew a woman wanted to hear. I whirled around, prepared to shove him off. But he didn't wear that giddy look of having provoked me to ire. He looked older and like something sad had happened to him, yet what had happened was that he'd asked at three months for me to end a pregnancy and then he left. Now that I'd met his wife, I understood why he'd done it. A child forced the marriage question, on which we'd been ambivalent; it'd been like flipping a coin to find out what you really wanted. When it landed, I'd been supposed to recognize the face he showed for the flipside, declare an accident a sign and fate out of our hands. He'd have stayed. It was just that my own mind hadn't stopped spinning and would not until the night, two months afterward, that my sister called about our parents. We hadn't spoken in weeks, not me and her, not me and them. Not out of animosity, but due to the sheer slipping of time.

He reached past me for my coat, the same as I'd had then, black double-breasted wool. I let him hold it while I fit in my arms, one then the other.

"It was nice meeting you," he said.

"Can you really keep this up?" I said. "I'm staying in that house until I die."

"Margaret calls ours a starter," he said flatly, without pride. When I raised my brows, he said, "It's her family's. The money."

I had never been one to run off right away. I snuck first up the stairs to see the boys. Each had his own room, a luxury my sister and I hadn't enjoyed. In our teenage years, our parents let us hang a curtain. She wore earplugs through my calls; I couldn't stand to see her studying. I wondered sometimes, still, in my bed in the house at the top of the hill, what I wouldn't give to have her, all three of them, just down the hall, to be somehow back at the beginning.

The night my sister called with the news, two months after A had left, I felt it in my gut, what I wanted. It wasn't simple, but I saw it clearly surfaced, reflecting in my mirror: it was to empty out my pockets of regrets, to collect no more. Or at least to call them something else.

Beaver's hair on the pillow was sheared close to his skull. I ran my palm over the texture. Wally's had grown into a trim and tidy 'fro. They both slept curled into balls, with parted lips. I was sorry I'd scared them, but some lessons you ought to learn soon as you can: never trust a woman once she's loved you. It's a spell whose breaking takes many tries; she'll think she's through, then call you back, conjure you up out of air. And at last, she'll do anything, just to be free.

"Dad?" Wally mumbled, but his eyes were shut. His father's voice had joined us on the second floor, murmuring to itself or on a call. I tucked the blankets to his ears, waiting till the coast was clear.

After the moving vans made the exchange complete, I stopped hiding my men, leading them by the hand down the street in broad day. Some wouldn't be seen to leave till Monday morning, when after a weekend of couples' card games and even-numbered dinner parties, Margaret A—— and Ward Cleaver—and I—went back to work. Not that my men and I were invited. We weren't even close to married, as I rarely bade any return.

I wound up once with one who could play. He lifted the lid and with his knuckles trilled the keys. The sound put the taste of Sunday morning on my tongue, the bacon burned, the pancakes golden, depending who took the bench, who took the griddle; always, my sister turned the sheets, I set the table on the beat. Not sure if I could take it, I went for air, gesturing that he go on, enjoy. The notes were muffled by the trees, amplified in the clearing. There, the A——s were immersed in picnicking. His wife was showing. I backed away. The curtains, I'd left drawn to the sun, the windows glinting, a bird broken already. At the piano, the man was in boxers and a dress shirt neatly pressed, the prematurely snow-white hair on his head disheveling again as he alternately rocked back and craned forth. Inside, I lay on the rug and listened with my eyes closed.

The baby was born by the night A climbed the stairs, in his old basketball shorts. He did what no other husband had ever done, which was to knock on my front door. I was alone, the cat bolting out past our planted feet.

"Why didn't you tell me?" he demanded. "Why didn't anyone get in touch?"

My parents—he'd never heard. When he left, they'd been in their prime, taking walks and eating healthy, but health has nothing to do with accidents, nothing to do with black ice and tipped-over tiny cars. Not one of our friends had known at first where he had gone—his own parents', of course; and he still had his same number.

I said I'd figured someone had. He said no, he'd distanced himself from all of them, shed anything resembling our shared life. June had brought it up that afternoon over brunch. I could see it, the four of them with cloth napkins on their laps, cold poached salmon and poached eggs. I turned, without shutting the door. He followed me inside.

Running his hand over the spines of my books, commenting on the papered walls: an assault on the eyes. I made tea, but he wanted a shot for it. On the couch we sat sipping, saying nothing, letting everything we felt fill the house until at last rose up that one thing left, the thing that so long carried us on. I tried to swallow it back with a swig from the bottle, but by then he'd said it: we'd never fucked in a house, only apartments.

I didn't think that it'd go on, that we would want it to,

but some edge had not been sewn and once you slipped back through, it opened wider and wider.

He took to taking morning hikes alone to catch the dawn. I'd rid my men before they fell into REM. I kept a light on and under the mat a key. For a while, Margaret was home on leave, nursing their child. I'd only seen it swaddled, in blue, when it was brought in from their SUV. He was clearly in thrall with it, the way his face now was always lit, but he was kind enough not to speak of it. To keep our pillow talk from our past or present circumstance, he told me of his suspicions that Ward was seeing someone in the city. I laughed it off, but he said he had an inside view. Now that his wife was back to work, he switched off with June on errands and babysitting. They'd become more than friends, more like confidants.

I put a hand on his thinning head of hair. "We should stop this."

"I know," he said, nuzzling my palm.

It was too late; we'd stitched ourselves back in: an airless pocket sealed from time, a private nesting apart from our separate realities. Mine, that I was alone. His, that he was theirs.

Yet even as we fell into old rhythms, pushing our doubts deeper down and the future farther on, and I cared less and less to keep up my liaisons, I recalled the urgency I had once felt alongside my grief: for my parents, for him, for the grandchild we could've given—motherhood the one shot that could've brought them all closer to me. It was the same urgency that had driven me, day after day, out of bed to face the mirror, the urgency that had led me to take the reins of where life was leading and buy the house. Letting go of what I'd had and hadn't had was only half; by the same token, no fulfillment of life, no possibility, was to be missed out on by default, by simply running out the biological clock. I did not regret any moment spent with him, but they did collect, and meanwhile the old maid was getting older.

We were being careful as you could be, more careful still than I had been with any other man or, before, with him; but if there was another accident, I didn't know if I could do it, not again, and knew neither could he.

The days lengthened as spring stretched into summer. June took to waiting for Ward on the front porch, tumbler in hand, the boys playing down at Eddie's. Seeing me she raised her glass, her heels kicked off to the grass. I would've been a suspect since I'd stopped flaunting my men, but I always turned the corner hours before his car arrived. Hefting the bag that held my laptop, I called, "We should do something sometime. Just you and me."

"And what do you propose we'd do?" she said, and laughed that white-toothed, crinkle-eyed laugh, rocking back in her chair. She was a beautiful woman, one who'd always held more sway than me, which was probably why we'd never spent much time as a pair. But now her powers had faded; with the right push she could be toppled. The thought both softened and frightened me. I saw that, in a deep way, we were enemies. If she ever had an inkling of me and A, she would destroy me.

Tilting her glass up to her lips, over the rim of it, she appraised the bag now cradled in a crook of my arm.

"Come by some night," she instructed, "when you haven't got any homework."

I said I would. But I never did, too busy.

Late August, the Cleaver boys were playing catch in the street. It was early evening, the twenty-third. Ward and Margaret were still at work; I newly arrived, looking down from my perch on the hill. When I'd passed the children by, they hadn't said hello, so immersed. The man who was and wasn't mine—who must've felt, both with and without me, with and without his wife, alone inside, unmendably, like us all—came out onto his lawn with his son strapped to his chest. The boys nodded in that ageless male manner of saying hello. He was good with them; they missed their dad, their mom as she had been: their dinners now defrosted from packages, spent TV-side. June was angled in her chair to face where the sun would set. Her view was of my house stripped bare, with all the curtains drawn. If she kept her gaze unsparing, let her mind clear of the drink, the truth would dawn, in the superimposition of a man running his way, as if beckoned, up the stairs.

For a while, A just stood there, watching the arc of the white ball from hand to mitt, the bouncing roll of it on cement. Then, from how his hands were set, held aloft, from the snap of his wrists, I knew that he had asked if they liked shooting hoops. Had Ward ever proposed it, June would've pointed out that by tacit accord, no one on our street, the whole neighborhood, had affixed a hoop to a garage, planted one at the curb in place of a tree. She would

never undermine the aesthetics of their house, their repu-
tation, purely in the name of recreation.

The boys must've expressed their interest, for he called
out next to June where she was sitting on the porch and,
after some conversation, handed the baby off to her. The
three then climbed into his SUV.

You can never really hurry an affair along, but that
meant, I told myself—knowing that it was, and just not
how, a lie—there was still time to turn this all around.
I should have just sat him down and said goodbye, our
damage to each other already done.

He took them, I later learned, to the next town's elementary, which had a painted playground court, and
there they stayed until twilight. He called his wife from
the car as they were pulling from the lot. Margaret and
Ward both had come home, she to an empty house, he
to an infant in his wife's arms: a reversal swiftly reme-
died. I poured a shot into my tea. Certainly A had not
been drinking, but he usually drove a little fast. Perhaps
the boys were bickering, and he turned in his seat. The
roads still new to him, the sharpness of the curve could've
come by surprise. The rail wasn't strong enough to hold
them in. They flew from the cliff and hit the water up-
side down. With my parents, it had been that the next car
couldn't stop, hitting that same patch of ice. With A and
the Cleaver boys, it was the door locks. Automatic.

The rumors started by the way I took the news, my
grief on a par with Margaret A——'s and the Cleavers'. I
called off from work and stayed in three weeks running,

the only one who didn't cook them casseroles or send them cards.

At the funerals we kept apart, I too bereft to play my part, they so bereft that they were blind, the only ones who couldn't guess. In the church, I sat in back near Ward's woman, a young June, with hair relaxed into waves and wearing flats instead of pumps. She might've given me a second look, but saw I was too old, too empty-eyed and incurious of her to pose a threat. She kept her sights on June, until by the caskets she crumpled; on Ward, until he went to his wife, crumpling too. At the A——s', I did my weeping on the bed with the coats—knowing someone from his side who'd traveled from the other coast might recognize me from a distant memory or from a picture—until some great-aunt of hers gave me a handkerchief and then the child. I held it listlessly, and it cried and wouldn't stop, its face blood-red and crumpling. The woman who lived on the corner, Eddie's mother, perhaps, took him away, saying maybe it was time I left.

It was Cliff who woke me to the whispering, though when I finally heard, it seemed for weeks there'd been a ringing. Suddenly the flashing lights that filled my dreams were sirens, had a sound.

"We know it's not your fault," he said over the phone, "but Clair and I think you should know what they've been saying."

As in, the others on the street, who had never been my friends. The way the children understood it, I'd cast a spell, laid a curse. They had no reason why; that was just how witches were. The parents were more scientific: I'd altered his state of mind. A newlywed father of a newborn had no business looking for excuse to leave the house. Although his phone had shown no evidence, going by the silent wife, they posited a call or text had come in at the crucial point: when the steering wheel should've been turning. Assuring them I'd been deleted long ago wouldn't help. I'd loved too much or not enough, and either way I had committed it without a thought. Still, there were some who didn't believe, who thought instead I must have lived in fantasy. That perhaps we had a past, but I'd not lured him back. Nothing but an old maid, making a spectacle of herself in borrowing from others' grief. My coveting was worse than theft, akin to killing in its desperation, its plea for attention.

And if any of them wondered, Cliff didn't say: not even Clair knew for sure I'd done it before. I might have confessed, had she needed me, but Clair, of course, had kept her baby.

It took only a month, my ear cupped to the glass, listening, as on the hillside stairs they passed. The Cleavers were already selling, going back to Ohio, where she'd grown up. They'd take her mom out of the home. There was no sign up at the A———s', but I knew she and the boy were gone and wouldn't return. Just one day a realtor would arrive, and a van of hired men.

I put the house up. The piano I was having shipped out to my sister. With some careful rearranging, it would fit in her one-room apartment. A crane came and lowered it down off the hill; all the children came to see, pointing as it tipped and skimmed the side. The cables righted not before a cake of mud sloughed from the earth, in crumbs, pebbles, and dust. Eddie peered up, pocketing a piece of debris that reached the street. Cloaked in curtain against the cold, I blew a breath, with my finger scrawled a name, and sleeved it off. It doesn't matter if it was mine or his or one that might've been. I told myself what I'd told myself once before and knew I'd never tell again: if it was to be a long life, the motions ought at least to keep the semblance of starting over.

CREATION STORY
\\\\\\\

THE LAST TIME THE CITY BURNED, my brother didn't stay for cake. Soon as we finished dinner, he pushed his chair out from the table and came back smelling of cologne. "I'm going out," he announced.

Dad glanced at Mom, who tried to keep her face from falling. She'd already pushed the candles in. Black cake showed in rings where each had plunged through the vanilla, like soil under snow. I'd been playing with the plastic lighter, but now Dad took it, tossed it down beside the stack of paper plates. "Out where?" he demanded.

"Out." Daniel scowled and drew his hood over his head, his parting gesture anytime he left the house. Dark fuzz lay like a shadow between his nose and lip. Around his neck a gold chain glinted. He'd told Mom it wasn't real, but I knew where he'd gotten it: at a pawnshop. The TV was on in the next room, and on the screen a news reporter wearing puffy gloves stood before a bungalow where flames licked out boarded windows. They cut to a helicopter shot of black smoke billowing from a forsaken factory I remembered seeing from the freeway.

Every birthday of my brother's life, the city burned, and our parents bade us stay in. When we were little, we made masks out of cardboard, painted to look tribal and fierce, and wore them watching from the window for suspicious activity. Specifically: people on foot, people with no business being here, darting stealthily between trees, carrying battered cans of gasoline. Our house was in a suburb seven miles from the city limits, and though we'd kept the cordless with us on the carpet, a girlish twin to Daniel's bat, we'd never had to dial 911. The next night we could celebrate; the next night was Halloween, and we'd be giddy, the neighborhood ours again. We roved the streets as rowdy bands of shiny, store-bought superheroes, clutching clean pillowcases full of loot.

This was what I thought of as tradition, but how long had it been like this? There was a gap between us of five years, a space that could have accommodated the birth of other siblings. In recent years Daniel sat sulking in the living room, sneaking out for surreptitious smokes, and I watched the street alone. Now he was sixteen, one step closer to adult. Looped on his thumb was a clinking new set of keys.

"Don't go anywhere stupid," Dad said, meaning south, into the city.

"There's only stupid places to go," Daniel muttered and banged out the door.

As Mom got up to watch the car back out of the driveway, I swiped a swoop of frosting from the cake. That afternoon I'd helped her bake it, piped the border on myself. More for us, then, I thought. By the time Mom returned, bolting the lock, Dad had punched the volume up and turned his chair.

Without looking at Mom or me, he said, "We should never have gotten him that car."

"Can I light them?" I asked.

IN LIFE YOU'RE RARELY GRANTED NOTICE that a year or night or instant will be a last, but looked at close, there're little ends. You only turn sixteen once.

That evening the TV droned. As on election night, they'd keep a count, and in the morning we would know the final score: how many fires had roared and structures been destroyed, how few culprits apprehended. The firefighters never won. They rushed to nearly every scene too late and while a dozen other vacant structures, miles apart, took a spark. Mom worked her needles at her knitting, growing a blanket in her lap. Dad sat jogging his foot in a steady constant beat, thrumming the couch. Trying not to mess up, I did my toes.

In the middle of the night I smelled him, the cologne just as strong as when he'd put in on, and yet it hovered

over some new, more pungent scent. I strain now to identify it. It wasn't weed or gasoline. I couldn't tell if his
murmuring with Dad down the hall was a fight. I was just
glad he hadn't ended up in jail or an accident.

In the morning I was running so far behind that Dad
threatened to leave me. I hadn't known what to expect
for the sixth grade, but after many consultations over the
phone the week before, I had confirmed it would be safe
to draw a pair of whiskers and black my nose, don a set of
ears—a black bodysuit and jeans being best underneath.

Daniel wasn't dressing up. He was in the same metal
band T-shirt that he wore twice a week. One of his eyes
had popped a vessel, the bloody fleck like a spattering
from somewhere else. "If you hurry, Beth," he said, "I'll
take you." A peace offering to us all.

"No, she's going with me," said Mom, the only one
who, if she wanted, if we didn't need groceries, could
spend the day in her pajamas. Dad and Daniel met eyes
briefly, as though only in passing milk for the cereal. It
was like her to take a burden on herself in punishment of
another. "I'll just be a minute," she said. "Finish my coffee and put on my face. Won't be cute as yours, Beth."

Once Dad and Daniel left, one car after the other, I
poked through the discarded paper. This year, in addition
to the totals, they had this figure: 34 percent of the city
touched by fires. That was the word, *touched*—as by an
angel—not *scorched*, not *consumed*, not *reduced to ash*. Remarkably, it stated, no one had died (apart from an unre-
lated east side homicide). *Can Only God Stop the Devil?* a
headline asked.

The statistics in the paper seemed to argue so, but already, behind the doors of a few small, private rooms, the solution must have been under discussion.

Mom was quiet on the way, absently tapping the horn in an assured succession of honks as we sped past the picketers outside the fence that wrapped the plant. The strikers raised their signs in an extension of their arms and waved to us.

When I enrolled in driver's ed, four years later, I'd be surprised this custom wasn't mentioned. Neither was the admonishment that, if you were going to cruise, at least cruise major strips, nor was the urban legend that a cop would never fault you for not stopping at a red light in the city, because it was safer not to, and cops had no time for such minor violations, anyway. Instead, they just warned that on the country roads, it was easy to forget how fast you're going.

"Your tail!" Mom exclaimed as I hopped out from the car. She thought I'd lost one.

"It's okay, Ma. Only skanks wear tails."

A SKANK WAS A GIRL who'd had sex more than once with more than one partner, or with one only once. By my own estimation, I was like any other middle-schooler, except I didn't do drugs and I didn't have sex at all. So far I'd roamed in packs so large it was easy to pretend I declined a pull or hit because I'd already had one. There wasn't much to go around. It was only October; we were still making our connections. On Fridays, we either went to Universal Skate or to the movies at the dead mall. I liked to think that Daniel was proud of me for fitting in, but I knew that at a certain point, fitting in would mean getting into trouble. Soon my friends would ask if I knew who could hook us up.

That night at the rink, they played Michael Jackson's "Thriller" and turned the lights down so the chemical inside our plastic necklaces would glow. A boy with a darker shadow between his nose and lip than Daniel's asked me for the second time to couples skate. Because I'd gotten out of it the week before by being in the restroom passing lip gloss with some girls, I said okay. His hand was slick with sweat, and as we took the curves, our arms pulled taut between us. Gliding past his friends who watched, one mouthed out, "Pussy."

When I got home, a few minutes shy of my 9:30 curfew, Daniel had just gone out. Dad was cracking a beer, Mom already sleeping in her chair.

"Did we get many trick-or-treaters?" I asked in hopes that there would be some candy left.

"The neighborhood's not what it used to be," Dad said ambiguously.

In the bathroom mirror, my whiskers had faded, but my nose was black. I missed Daniel like he'd been gone for years already.

EACH YEAR BEFORE THE SNOW FELL, and for some time after, the city worked on demolition. What hadn't burned to a foundation would be leveled and, with the spring, would rise up saplings. Long stripped of copper, buildings awaiting final destruction were further pillaged for metal scrap by roaming pickups. The only way the city could afford to pay for bulldozers and wrecking balls was through an annual federal grant.

"It's disgusting," Mom said one night, turning off the TV as we all sat down to dinner. "Instead of giving us this grant, they should apply more to social services. Food stamps. Planned Parenthood."

"Balance the budget," said Dad, who was less liberal.

"Defense," Daniel said definitively beneath his hood. He had taken to wearing it even before he went outside. We all looked up from our plates in surprise. "Tanks, right? Bombs. Uzis. Agent Orange. Think of all the foreign civilians we could be killing."

"Daniel," Mom said in disappointment, but I liked where he was going.

"Yeah," I said. "If we take all the abandoned buildings away, where is anyone supposed to smoke their crack?"

"Elizabeth," Mom said, with a clink setting her fork. Dad had stopped chewing, the food paused in his mouth. Daniel started laughing so hard he had to spit his food into a napkin.

"What *is* this?" he said, examining the masticated bolus.

"I thought we'd try the generic," Mom said, sounding hurt. "I didn't think you'd notice."

The cordless rang. Dad handed it off without saying hello. "Tell your friends to stop calling during dinner."

I took it down the hall. Daniel never got calls because

he had a pager. It was Meadow. In elementary she'd been called Cindy and gone home with lice, and now, with her ratted hair, she'd come out on top. Nobody knew which was her real name.

"I heard you won't skate again with Jay." She paused to crack her gum. "Don't you like him?"

"I don't know," I said. I couldn't tell if she was asking because she did. I took the risk that either way would gain me points. "I guess."

The line crackled in the quiet, Meadow snapping her gum. Then the real occasion for her call was introduced. "Some of us have been wondering," she began. "Couldn't your brother hook us up?"

ON SATURDAYS DANIEL DIDN'T GET UP until one. By then I'd finished with my homework, even with the TV on. First he'd pour himself a bowl of cereal so he could gather strength enough to make a fast food run. This particular afternoon, Mom was at a baby shower, and Dad was out raking leaves. We couldn't see him where we sat, but we heard the endless scraping of the rake. When we were little, we would have gone to jump in the pile, Daniel face-first, grabbing a fistful for my head. Through the blaring of commercials, I felt our silence. I turned to him and asked straight-out. I said it wasn't for me.

"Why do you think I could get it?" he said, flashing a grin that showed his filling then quickly faded. He got up and rinsed his bowl, leaving it for Mom to load in the dishwasher. He came back in a hoodie and jeans that hung so low they showed his boxers. I picked the polish from my toes as he studied me over me the sink.

"I'm not gonna do it. You're innocent. You're gonna stay that way if I can help it."

He said it like a promise, and I would have been relieved had I not known what sight I'd see at school on Monday morning, the consequence of failing Meadow: her brushing past me in the hall, Jay towed close behind with a finger hooked in her belt. It wasn't him, but what it'd stand for.

"Hey," said Daniel. "I'm hitting Telly's—how many sliders can you eat?"

Innocence gets shed in fluffs, sudden then steady, as by a shearing. It was that night, of the first fleeting flurries that didn't even slick the streets, that my brother was arrested. The final charge would be trespassing, not possession. Downtown at the courthouse, the cop would say to our parents, "We can tell he's a good kid. What's he doing wearing all those baggy clothes?"

FOR OVER A MONTH, my brother didn't come to the table. Evenings and weekends were spent in his room, his car parked beneath the maple, battered first by the last of the leaves, and then blanketed by snow. He didn't even join us at Thanksgiving, when we drove upstate to our cousins', the freeways ceding to a highway then to a maze-like turning of dirt roads. Our hippie uncle, who organic farmed and left his sheep out in the cold because they did it in New Zealand, chuckled and referred to our parents' days in reggae clubs, but Mom got tight-lipped and Dad told him Daniel was the one being so hard on himself. He wasn't grounded from dinner or family events.

"It was just pot?" asked my cousins, who were Daniel's age and a year and a half younger. We all wore jeans, but I felt self-conscious in my scoop-necked bodysuit, and cold any time we were six feet from the wood-burning stove. They had on flannels and frayed sweaters from the thrift store, both because and not because it was cool. Their Timberlands sat in the mudroom, functional for the farm.

"It's my parents," I said. "They took away his car."

"That sucks," said Philip. "At least he gets one," added Anna. "I know!" I said, like he was the only one of us two who got spoiled. In the kitchen their mother was kneading bread, while mine was popping open fancy wine.

He gave in for Christmas over at Grandma's, her whole house sparkling in tinsel and lights, smelling of honey ham and marshmallows, an angel blank of facial features atop the tree. Among his gifts was a set of shiny rims I'd helped my parents pick. "Thanks," he muttered in their direction. He still had a couple weeks more to ride out on his punishment and hadn't gotten them or me anything. He sat and watched while Mom gathered up the paper at his feet, until Grandma asked if our arms were broken. Then even Dad put down his new handheld blackjack game to help.

"Sorry, Grammie," I said, kissing her on her head, dyed to match mine and Mom's. "Just be good to your mother," she said, holding her neck up stiffly. "Then no one needs to be making apologies."

After we ate and everyone was milling around before dessert, I put my coat on and followed Daniel to the porch like I couldn't stand it any more than he could. Mostly he held the cigarette and watched it drifting smoke.

"I owe you," he said. "I couldn't get to the store."

"It's okay," I said. I was jumping on Grandma's shoveled steps to keep warm, feeling proud for not coughing from the smell. Meadow had caught me fake-inhaling from a cigarette she'd stolen from her mom's purse expressly for me, and before her teasing got too mean, I'd told her how my grandpa died of cancer and emphysema. "Aw," she'd said, briskly rubbing my back. Her mood set the temperature of our crowd, and we'd been on shaky ground since she'd started going with Jay.

"It's not okay." Daniel turned, stubbing out the cigarette. In the grayness of the day, his eyes looked dark as a basement. In the sun they flickered between brown and green. "I want to give you something really awesome, something that even if you grow out of, you'll always remember."

I clutched my coat close, smiling, almost afraid to show the way warmth flooded my chest. Afraid because he was my brother, so I maybe shouldn't have held him so much higher than all others. No boy who asked me to skate made me feel anything but sealed-up like a block of ice.

AFTER THE NEW YEAR, the city council had a look at the proposal, put together by the mayor's office on the advice of several independent contractors. They compared it to the budget and held a quick and quiet vote. The solution was that the demolition, paused by the subzero temps in winter, wouldn't stop. Instead it would take a brief hiatus, pick back up in spring, and ratchet into summer. By Devil's Night, the arsonists, the addicts, the vandals, the murderers, all would have to call a new place home.

The day we heard that the entire city was going to be razed, top to bottom, every corner, even along its borders shared with suburbs—no square inch spared—my brother wasn't with us. Part of his truce with Mom and Dad was getting a job and using it to pay his fine and the note on his car. He delivered pizzas three nights a week and always smelled of it, the garlicky tomato sauce and pepperoni.

The press conference they were playing seemed historic, so I jumped up from the dinner table and hit record to get it on the empty tape we kept inside the VCR. But everyone already knew: the newscast had run as live early that morning. Dad pointed to the evening paper, and there it was, on the front page. *City Declared DOA*, it said big above the fold, *Remains to Follow Jobs, Ship Overseas.* Beneath began a two-page urban history, tracking the city from its beginnings as a fort to its postwar population height and subsequent steep decline. An editorial, repurposing the city's official motto, was titled, *We Hope for Better Things; Shall They Rise from the Ashes?*

No one had told me. Not during breakfast, when I'd been fussing with the tight roll on my jeans. All day at school it'd not been mentioned, not by one teacher in any class. Meadow had been crying in the bathroom, over a fight with Jay, and I'd sat on the sink, just listening.

"A long time coming, I suppose," said Mom, whose parents grew up in the city and left for the suburban plant, just built. Her voice was distant and dry, as though carried on a wind.

"Same way they handle wildfires," said Dad. "Make a control line. Remove the kindling."

A map was shown on the screen, with arrows indicating the plan of attack: they would start from the north, the east and west, and work their way in, down to the river. The wreckage would be sent on a barge out to sea. Much of the scrap would go to China.

"But it can't all be empty," I said.

The mayor concluded his remarks and stepped back from the mic. The room exploded in shouting. Reporters waved their hands and raised their fists, stood on top their seats. One stood still then tore his press badge off, kicked his folding chair flat, and held it high to rush the podium. The screen went black and returned to a white-faced anchor, whose partner held between her decaled nails a shaking sheet of paper. "You heard it," he said, seeming to fumble for words. "There just aren't enough residents. Those tens of thousands will be displaced."

"Turn it off," Mom said in disgust. Dad turned it off. With a whir, the VCR stopped recording.

I'D BEEN ASLEEP ABOUT AN HOUR, not yet dreaming of anything, when a mix of pizza delivery and cologne flooded my room. Daniel was standing above me, hood over his head. "Get dressed," he said. "Come with me."

My only hesitation was in what to put on. My heart

beat wildly. Finally I chose a hoodie I hadn't worn since the year before, in elementary. For jeans I kept my usual, tight-rolled and slim-fitting.

I followed him to his car, which he'd parked far from the maple, off down the street. I made the same steps as he and missed the worst of the mud and melting ice.

I trusted Daniel. When he was born, I was five years from existing. I've often wondered, why are we more terrified to think of dying than to contemplate how we once just did not exist? They are the same. Maybe because death can be so sudden, the person disappeared but the body lingering, whereas coming into being is a slow process, cell by cell. My brother had always been there. He'd shown me what it was to deal with Mom and Dad. That night, he showed me the city.

"Buckle up," he said. He wouldn't start the car until I did. Crumpled fast food bags and empty Mountain Dews littered the floor. He pressed play on a mix tape that was part metal, part rap, and we exited the subdivision, passed through the stoplights heading to the entrance ramp, and wound our way up to the freeway. The southbound lanes were fast and empty. It was like traveling through outer space with billboards.

Without turning the music down, he told me how, a few hours before, he'd been held up for his tips at gunpoint. He was delivering to an apartment that was the kind with stairs outside, like an extended-stay motel. "I was creeped out even before I saw the barrel."

The gun greeted him at the door. The guy was short and wearing a knit cap and diamond earrings. He grabbed Daniel by the collar and yanked him inside, leaving the door open wide. Daniel wasn't going to make a sound, and no one was walking by. The apartment was dark except for a fish tank lit by fluorescents, and cloudy with marijuana.

"I was like, dude! I've got a joint and enough to make change for a twenty—that's *it*. He sure got his pizza free."

Hearing it as a story made it unreal. I wondered if to Daniel it had felt any less like a movie or a dream. He wasn't acting like it. He cracked the window and, with his knee against the wheel, lit up a cigarette.

"He was pointing the gun the whole time?" I was embarrassed of my voice, which sounded shrill and disbelieving, like Mom's when she was upset. "Did he have it to your head?"

"Nah. It was down by his side. He just wanted me to know it was there."

The guy also took his keys. He pushed Daniel from the apartment and tossed them over the rail. They hit metal, then the asphalt. When the door slammed shut, the number blurred into nothing. It was on the order, but Daniel didn't want to remember. He was late getting back because in the dark it took a long time to find his keys.

"I'm fired," he said and shrugged.

"Can they do that? What did the cops say?" Daniel looked over, one hand on the wheel, his expression patient and pitying. I steadied my voice the way I had to when I was called on in class. "Didn't you have to make a report?"

"Why give police the satisfaction?" Before I could ask what he meant, Daniel added, "The guy was black."

That got me quiet. I'd thought we weren't supposed to

talk about that, the color that someone's skin happened to be. On either side of us, dilapidated homes bore down. The freeway, elevated in the suburbs, had receded below the level of the street. Off in the distance, the tall buildings of downtown shone metallic. Few lights were on in the offices. The electric bill would be enormous, just to set aglow the vacant floors.

Daniel veered off right for an exit. The residential streets were empty, storefronts on the corners graffitied, sidewalks cracked with weeds and glittering with broken glass.

"Doesn't anybody live around here?" I asked.

He glanced over. "Of course." His eyes were dark, but as we passed beneath a working streetlamp, I saw them flickering brown-green. "Look, forget I ever told you. I'm fine. I'm free. This'll be fun. This is an adventure."

The train station stood alone, towering almost as a rampart, in fortification of itself. Its beaux-arts facade, columned and arched, was the only part that looked 3-D. We parked around the back, outside the fence that marked it off. There, the barbed wire hung loose and looping from the side. Everywhere, signs told us to stay out, warned of guard dogs and video cameras. I pointed one out and almost tripped on a crumbling of bricks that seemed to have been dumped from somewhere else.

"You see any cameras?" Daniel said. I smiled and shook my head. "Hear any barking dogs?" I tipped my head back to the moon, a waxing gibbous. At school we'd been studying the phases. "Woo-woooo," I called out softly. Daniel laughed and climbed up first. With a hand out to bolster me, he helped me down. For some reason, I didn't wonder about where and how he'd been caught before, what would happen if he got caught making trouble again.

I don't know what I thought we'd find inside. A party. Electronic music we somehow hadn't heard or felt. A circle of friends Daniel knew well, a secret girlfriend who'd look upon me as her own relation. He'd make the introductions, and I wouldn't have to do a thing I didn't want. I'd be a little sister, off-limits, safe.

We stepped through a gaping absence where there might once have been a door. It was like a cathedral or some place in Europe: the vaulted ceiling, the mosaic tile work. Daniel shone a flashlight around. Puddles potted the marble floor from snow that'd blown in and melted. It was holy in a human way; you lit candles not to talk to God but for company. The vastness seemed to contain something lonely and eternal—not ghosts or memories, but maybe time, if it could keep a pulse. And if the beating could accrue, with no one living it. Daniel touched my shoulder so as not to startle me when he cupped his hands around his mouth and hollered out, "Hellooo!" His voice echoed into the void until it stopped sounding like him. When I raised my hands to do the same, he thrust a hand to stay me. "Just listen."

Nothing. No: Water dripping in syncopated rhythms. In some dank depth, an animal scuttering. Through the absence where a door had been, the whistling wind.

THAT WEEK AT SCHOOL, I held the secret of what Daniel had shown me inside like a new dimension—one that, because I had it hidden from everyone else, remained a mystery even to myself. Friday I went with my pack of friends straight from school to a triple feature, which entailed buying tickets for one show and slipping in to two more. Already, they cost only a dollar-fifty. The first was half cartoon, half reality, one we'd all seen before; the second was a horror flick I fell asleep for. When I woke, they'd all left me for another row, snickering. I pretended not to care, moving to sit beside them, crossing my legs. Meadow had said all us girls would wear skirts, but when we got there, everyone else'd changed into jeans. The third was about a man obsessed with a teenage girl and had a fingering scene on a rollercoaster.

At nine Meadow said we had more time before her mom would pick us up. I was not supposed to leave the theater, in the west wing of the mall. The only operational anchor store was just closing at the other end of the mall, but the ice cream shop and the arcade in the middle were, like the movies, open late. I foresaw that even if I got dropped off first, I'd miss my curfew, and I felt a kind of drifting, like when I squeezed my legs at night beneath the sheets.

The deadness of a dead mall after close was no more than during the day. Passing the rows of for-lease stores, their illumined emptiness beyond the rolling gates, there was a sense we owned it all. When we came to one gaping partway open to a darkness, Meadow dared someone to go inside. I surprised them all by squatting down in my skirt and ducking in. Jay's friend Kyle, who had spiky hair and preferred skateboards to skates, followed behind. The yellow sale signs were still up on the walls: 70% off, no returns. The racks displayed no merchandise, merely skeletons. Kyle spun one around like they were dancing. Then he kicked it down. Behind the counter, his hand brushed my skirt. I knew that he wanted to reenact what we'd seen on the screen.

At first I was ice, and just when I began to feel more like a floe, a gliding over, a series of pops sounded out in the mall, followed by screams.

"Get down!" Kyle cried hoarsely. His hand was gone so fast, pulling me to the floor, it was like it'd never been there. Already, I knew it'd never be again.

"Fuck! That was a fucking gun!" We heard Meadow amid the other, more girlish shrieks of our friends, Jay's high and cracking.

We waited under the counter, not talking, until a rent-a-cop came to clear the scene. Bullets had only shot up toward the ceiling. It'd been a gang. "That was weird," Kyle kept saying as we speedwalked to the theater, a foot apart. "I wasn't really scared, though." I stayed quiet, wondering was this what Daniel had felt, just before he'd been arrested—exhilarated and invincible, because of danger, not despite it. Was this the lesson he'd tried to teach me in telling me about his mugging, in taking me to the city— when I'd felt snug beneath his wing, safe because he had been saved? That for a minute, your life could feel more real than anything that was happening. Usually I felt the opposite. I'd been far from Kyle even as he touched me, and the shots woke us up. We'd been playacting: me no better than a mannequin, he that that could ever fake fun or carelessness well enough.

We caught up with Meadow and the others as her mom was pulling up, and I got in at 10:10: Dad the one asleep in the chair, Mom rinsing cans out at the sink for the deposit. She didn't look at the clock.

"Your father lost his job today," she said. "The company's going under."

"Oh," I said, and as she didn't explain what this meant for tomorrow's dinner, or my field trip next week, or our summer vacation to see Dad's parents in Florida, I asked, "Where's Daniel?"

"I guess he got the pizza place to take him back." She turned the tap off and came and hugged me, her breasts soft inside her sweater, her frizzy hair scratching my neck. I felt she could smell everything, but her embrace was as complete as it'd ever been. "Watch TV with me, Beth. Keep me company."

WE WATCHED NIGHT AFTER NIGHT that spring into summer. Helicopter shots showed the city shrinking in wide swathes from all three sides, a large-scale mowing. On the empty acres, they were going to be planting corn, plus a few small organic farms, an apple orchard. The center from which we'd spun would be the country. Like my hippie uncle, we were getting back to basics.

"So we'll drive Japanese cars? Or horses and buggies?" said Daniel, heading out in his hoodie. The nametag attached low, to its pocket, read simply *Dan*, but the letters had been scratched to spell out *Dawg*. I doubted he had told the pizza place about his mugging, but I didn't know for sure. Just as though he could sense somehow my need to digest alone what had happened at the mall, we hadn't seen each other much lately.

"Finally, we're hiring!" Dad mocked the evening news from his chair, sipping beer. Not many locals took the jobs on wrecking crews. Most had come from the rural south and Mexico.

Officials were giving housing vouchers to the homeless and the soon-to-be displaced, but instead of moving to a suburb where no one wanted them (flashes of protests, thrown rocks), many were just packing up and squatting deeper in the city. They cleaved closer and tighter to the heart. Tents sprung up in vacant lots, fires burned in barrels. Together, people cooked, barbecue and pots of beans. At night they danced in the street. Anyone who laid themselves on the ground before their house, their business, was picked up and forcibly removed by police. An old man doused himself in gasoline and lit himself with a match. The living room was stiff and silent. I had to talk about it all with someone. I called Meadow.

I remember as I was hanging up the phone one night Daniel hadn't had to work, he'd thrown open his door. "Don't *talk* to that girl anymore."

I whirled around. He was angry, white-knuckled where he held the jamb, his hood slipped off his head. "What? Why?"

"Don't think I can't hear your inane conversations. You're smarter than that." He slammed the door shut in my face. *That* made me cry, not the man engulfed in flames. Not the way, once he'd been toppled and clapped out, strips of skin hung from him, black, and pink underneath.

Later I got that my friendship with Meadow and the others had been doomed from the start, but for a long time afterward I told myself it was because Daniel had asked that we'd stopped hanging out.

One of the last nights we all met up at Universal was for my birthday in July. Daniel surprised us rink-side with a stack of pizzas—his way of telling me, I guess, we could be as close again as we'd been that night in the city, when he'd taken the shears to my innocence himself and tried to prune it gently back. From his pocket he produced a gold charm bracelet, dangling dice and baby shoes. He clasped it to my wrist and walked off, jeans slipping down past his boxers. "Oh my god!" my girlfriends squealed. "Your brother is *such* a baller."

It was then, I thought, I'd stopped being forgiven for standing on the edge of what everyone else was doing. With a brother like him, I should have been more at ease with them. Kyle must've never told them I was a skank.

BY LATE SUMMER, crews were closing in on the center. All the displaced who hadn't left were gathered in the park on the riverfront. Different groups had organized and pooled their guns, built stockpiles of rubble. It wasn't families anymore, no single mothers with kids; they all had gone. It was men, mostly, mostly young. Routinely raided and searched, they held their hands up in the air, got slammed down on the ground.

"They've got to learn," Dad said at dinner, not without regret. "This can't be stopped. No one can admit till something's done it wasn't right—just look back at history."

"What if that was me?" Daniel demanded.

"It's not," Mom said quietly. I knew why it couldn't be, and that the shame for what we were and hadn't chosen, but still would choose, caught in our throats, was the real reason we didn't speak. We scraped our forks along our plates and refused to meet his eyes, setting on us each in turn.

Our relief that Daniel was with us was cause enough for him to take off in his car. After all, he was nearly seventeen. But there was more. All his life, my brother must have felt that same flickering heat of a city set aflame inside him. Maybe, simply, Daniel didn't see himself as outside it. Maybe the burning was misunderstood; it wasn't just rage or rebellion, but vitality, a light. He stepped inside the hollowed train station, plumbed gutted factories with his beam, for more than the thrill, the risk: to call out, in his own way, those who kept away, precisely in search of what, exactly, those signs and fences named unsafe. Those buildings once were filled and stood as proof that shoulders brushed, and they were being sacrificed. Year after year, the burning rose in intensity: *See me. I'm hungry. I'm alive.*

THE NIGHT BEFORE SCHOOL WAS set to start—Daniel's senior year, and for me, seventh grade—cameras were standing by to film the final raid. Filling airtime, they interviewed one man, middle-aged, who said he'd been a felon and lost everything he had long before he lost his halfway house, his job washing dishes in a downtown Coney dog joint. The TV cut to a rolling tank, crushing the debris of some anonymous part of the city that might've been mere blocks or miles away. It could've been anywhere, another country. Inside, the park was bristling with young men who paced, touching their waistbands, lifting the caps from their heads to swipe at sweat. They broke from huddles to show the camera stores of brick, broken cement; on one such pile sat a young woman with eyes that seemed to glint back gold. Along the park peripheries, cops were lining up in riot gear, their shields one enormous wall.

Daniel stood by the door. A separate patch of dark hair had grown in on his chin. He said, "I'm going."

We all knew what he meant. He suddenly seemed to have been waiting for just this. I sat between Mom and Dad, frozen on the couch, Mom's knitted blanket draped on our laps. Dad's leg stopped jogging. Mom set down her glass of wine. Nobody could think of what to say to stop him. Only once the door had softly shut did my heart leap with delinquent replies: hide his keys, slash his tires. My parents should've never gotten him that car.

Mom ran from the room with a hand on her mouth. Without a look or a word, Dad passed his beer to share, and I held it without sipping. We watched the crowd surge forth from the park, flooding the empty streets. We watched as a rock was thrown, and then a brick. The wall of shields pushed in, closing the space between. A policeman shot the first fizzing canister into the swarm, sending up a cloud of gas. A face streamed tears.

Teenagers, I understand, still drive the dirt roads on starry nights, looking for a lost tribe who'd learned to live off the land. At eleven, at twelve, I believed in afterlife, an up above or down below. People had to end up somewhere. They didn't just disappear.

My brother was amongst those smoked out into the wasteland, where cops were waiting with their paddy wagons and their sticks. In the chaos, some managed to fan out and find refuge in the wreckage. Eventually, it all was gone, and in its place acre after acre of rowed-up corn.

EVERY GOOD MARRIAGE
BEGINS IN TEARS
\\\\\\\

I HAVE FOUND HER. The girl who will marry me.

At the vodka stand the girl tilts the bottle, pouring into paper cups. Hair falls before her face. Her skin looks raw from exposure to the cool spring air. Shaky, unsure, she spills a little on the counter. The red-nosed man waiting cries, "I'm not paying for that! Go on, fill it up, to the top!"

I try to meet her eyes to offer a kind smile, but even as it comes my turn and I order a shot, take it down, and receive my change from the familiar, older girl she works beside, she doesn't look up once. She is already used to pushy, alcoholic men, and she is not easy. She knows how to slip away and be forgotten. She belongs to no one.

"Another for you?" says the older, nasal and insistent.

I shake my head, but linger. The liquor has balanced the weight held in my chest. I feel light. The mussiness of the girl's dark, falling hair reminds me of Zarina; but, shy, aloof, with a look of serious concentration, she is nothing like her.

When I leave the library after a day spent in silence, I normally find the noise and motion of the streets a welcome change. I let my body be picked up by the crowds and wander the market square, examining the wares and buying what I suspect Mother may need for the meal. But today, I went straight for the vodka stand. Bodies pressed at my back, and each shoulder that smacked against mine as I passed made me ready for a fight. Yet every time I turned to confront the offender, he was far behind, absorbed in himself. My family's questions of me these months past, their gentle insistence, came like knocks echoing in my head. Even Zarina wanted to know. Then, like the simplest answer, there she was.

"Is this your young sister?" I ask. "You worked alone before."

The older girl calls forth the next order, then says, "Sorry she's so slow, but she's in training. Our father plans to open one more stand."

"Is vodka a good business?"

"Excuse me?" She is getting impatient. I order another shot, tip it back.

"What is her name?" My words come out cold, like a demand, and at last the young girl, shyly, looks at me. Small, she has a round but delicate face, more Russian-looking than Mongolian or Chinese, and alert, intelligent eyes. She seems somehow wise and innocent at once. She can't be older than sixteen. It may be the liquor or my own lust, but it seems as though, in our shared glance, the briefest courtship has taken place: my open interest, her acceptance of it.

"Her name is Aigul. And I," the sister says, hardening her eyes, "am Nazgul."

I realize she's no fool. To steal this young girl and earn her heart, I must be wary of the older. I know because I have Kuban. That is the way of siblings, who knew love as loyalty before they knew lust. I crumple my paper cups and rejoin the crowd, folding in this time like part of the cloth.

FOR MONTHS MY BROTHER, Kuban, has been saying, *Now, Bakyt, it's your turn. You will see, marriage is a kind of bliss. Come to me when you're ready. Me and the boys. We will all go together, just like the last time. We will help you go get her.*

His own bride was easy to capture, for she wanted to be caught. From the market square, she walked her usual route, swinging carefree a basket of unsold rolls, dark hair riding her back like something warm and alive. Girls do not normally walk alone so late. Over their short months of courtship, Kuban often saw her safely home. He knew the way well. We kept a fair distance as we followed behind. When she disappeared into a gated courtyard, Kuban directed me, his chosen driver, to the shortcut's other side.

I killed the headlights, and Usen and Azamat passed

the vodka. Drink, we'd been told, would put everyone in good cheer, bring bravery to the core of our stomachs, steady and strengthen our hands. Doubtless I was the only one who needed it. At the bar, in the closing hours of the afternoon, I'd been among the loudest and most assured. "Brother!" I'd cried, again and again. "You make me so proud!" When we left, a soberness had taken over, even though I knew that, as the driver, I would not have to help. Azamat offered to take my place at the wheel.

"You, Azamat, is this some joke? You know I don't trust you with my car."

Kuban pointed the boys to the back. "I want my big brother up front, by my side."

Likely, they all knew the truth: I was afraid. Afraid to take part, and afraid to relinquish my brother to his bride. Our new government has made a law against what we were about to do. The act, officially, is under all circumstance illegal, as it was under the Soviets—though far more common now. I've heard of no prosecutions. Usen and Azamat were always up to break the law. Kuban was not so easily led, but he liked of the four of us to be first, never mind it was a risk to take a wife. To me he just seemed to be following the new trend, which was revival of an old tradition. I didn't otherwise understand why my young brother, with whom I'd gone to the whorehouse, sharing old girls and looking out for new ones, now wished to be married, to be bound in this way.

The floor of dusk dropped out, plunging us into night, and Zarina's fine form appeared at the courtyard gate. She lingered a moment, squinting against the glow of the lamp, then crossed into the street before us. In a trick of the dark, the ground swallowed her feet and her white dress glided through air. Kuban's girl became a mysterious creature, unknown even to himself.

"She's beautiful," he whispered, and I too was seduced by the seeming magic in that moment. It felt nothing like I had expected. I could suddenly see why he would let her take him over, why she would lead and he would follow.

With the wheel gripped between my hands, and my brother's happiness beside me, I crept the car along behind Zarina. Her ghostly image, so eternal, brought a new thought to mind. Tradition was a rope thrown out by our ancestors, and we had caught it and held firm, as they trusted we would. Tied to the past, we were drawn back into it, made ancient—all those hands gripping the same long rope. We tugged and pushed forward, bringing our ancestors along, and when the time came, I knew then, I'd throw the rope out myself.

We came to a stop once we reached an empty street. It was unlikely that others would interfere, but Kuban didn't want an audience. Usen and Azamat tumbled out their car doors and stood hitting one another's back, puffing out their breaths in clouds. In respect for Kuban on his special night, they'd been abnormally quiet, exchanging smiles I spied in the rearview. My brother leaned in as if to plant a kiss, and I smelled the clean vodka, like something holy, on his breath. I read clearly an animal thrill in his eyes.

"Keep the engine running," was all he said, and I hadn't time to say, with new solemnity, "Make me proud, brother," before he sprinted down the street after his bride, Usen and Azamat in close pursuit.

The three caught her under a streetlamp. Kuban tackled her to the ground, and Azamat helped to hold her down, clasping her wrists so Usen could tie them. Her screams came in short, even bursts, likely practiced, and Kuban gagged her mouth to silence them. He held Zarina under her arms; Usen picked up her feet. She squirmed only a little. As they carried her body to the car, my brother peered into her eyes and she stared back. I can't pretend to know what was communicated, but I wonder if the look was meant to give one another a last chance. That's the kind of respectful relationship they seemed to have. But even if he had let her drop to run, Usen and Azamat, misunderstanding, would have dragged her right back. I would have told my brother later, *That was a close call. We almost lost her.*

There was a clump and a slam from the back, and then the boys were in the car. I hit the gas but was careful to take the turns slow. Zarina's feet kicked against the trunk, and I held my tongue from asking if that was necessary. My car was old, already in bad shape, the only one between us. A gift from Father, years ago, which I've not repaid—it was understood that I would drive it to a job.

When we drove past the bar, Azamat hooted to the men outside. Kuban was strangely silent. Usen cried out the name of our young nation. The men shouted it back and shook their heads, forgiving themselves for joining our rowdiness. We had drunk with these men, they'd offered their advice, and they knew we now had Zarina.

At the house, Mother tried to play her part and look stern yet reassuring, but there were tears of joy in her eyes. Father helped us settle Zarina into a chair and did the untying. She blinked in the brightness of the kitchen but didn't speak. She would look only at Mother, who placed a cup of steaming tea into her hands.

"You know why you're here," Mother said to Zarina, smoothing her mussed, dark, lovely hair.

Usen and Azamat stood back as if guarding the door. Kuban held his head low. I couldn't see his face. Mother retrieved the *jooluk*, and Zarina accepted the scarf's placement on her head. There was a strange moment when it seemed no one knew what to do next, as though a heaviness were keeping each of us to ourselves. At last Zarina's parents arrived with many more bottles of vodka and a cake. The feeling lifted, and our faces joined in celebration.

Kuban took Zarina into his room that night, and in the morning they emerged, shy and happy, a married couple.

IN THE MONTHS SINCE WE STOLE ZARINA into our home, she has brought to it a sweet newness. Mother has someone to help her in the kitchen and seems renewed of energy, and even Father has been caught smiling. Kuban no longer joins us for drinks at the bar, and in his fulfilling happiness, he has no need for the whorehouse. I have little patience for Usen and Azamat alone, the whorehouse of my memory has become sad and false, and I'm home more often too. Our walls are now filled with communal laughter, when it used to be so quiet, Kuban and me silent allies against Father's rebukes and Mother's loyalty to his side.

Through the walls, night after night, I can hear Kuban's panting and Zarina's drawn-out moans. Soon she will be showing, and within the year, our home will be changed even more. Yet I don't find myself dreading this. The image gives me unexpected pleasure: a wailing child in Zarina's arms and on her face a new smile, subtle and content—different from the one she gives to Kuban.

My family's questions have not ceased since the happy marriage. Kuban has been asking, *Don't you want a warm bed? Don't you want a woman of your own?* Zarina adds, *Don't you want a sister for me?* Mother has been saying, *Who will take care of you when I'm gone? Who will make you* borsok *the way you like?*

Father is the only one silent on the subject. He long ago gave up on me. I'm getting too old to not be married, and it's worse now that Kuban has found his wife. Father must expect that I will be the type who forever hangs around, hoping to inherit his desk. Our new government is just as crooked as the old, but Father's good job does not leave the family in want and has saved Kuban and me from a life in factories. Kuban delivers memoranda by bicycle and has been promised a career stacked with promotions. Father believes my insistent unemployment shows a lack of appreciation. We try to arrange our schedules out of sync, but the morning after I find Aigul—dawdling and dreamy, with my answer to them all, her name, on the tip of my tongue—I bump him from behind the newspaper.

The night before, the kitchen too quickly cleared, Zarina and Kuban took a long dusklit walk alone, and I had no one to tell of her. With Father, the old argument begins again, as though nothing could be new.

He says kindly, but with force, "Come with me today. I'll see you have that interview." He has in mind some basement filing job or another.

"I have plans," I say. I prefer to continue my private studies at the library. I began them years ago, with an interest in Europe, a region that knows its past, yet has a place in the future. I've let curiosity guide these studies, reading up on customs, trade, and revolutions, but lately I've become lost in my own country's history. It's no wonder the world has forgotten us. Our mountains sheltered us from sight when they couldn't stop us being conquered. Once a tribal people, free nomads and shamans, we were shown Islam, organized into farms, made part of an empire, more than once. After centuries oppressed, we barely remember ourselves. It's important, I believe now, we rediscover who we are, our traditions, before building something new.

Father doesn't believe in shortcuts, and education, to him, is the worst kind of shortcut, an assumption that you deserve to know more than you have need of. He would deny how old-fashioned and Soviet this sounds, arguing there's just no reading ahead; the man on top, the boss, will be the one to grant your path in accordance to a greater map.

"Plans?" he says. "What you have is a stubborn nature, not plans. It's time for you to pull your own weight.

You know it's not so easy to get an interview, and still, you have to prove yourself alone."

"I know that. I don't ask for your help."

His face goes dark and disappointed, yet he must be in no mood for a fight. When Zarina interrupts, "Father, would you like more tea?" he only says, "If it's hot."

Zarina has never served his tea lukewarm and makes it just as strong as he likes, stronger than her own husband prefers. She doesn't meet my eyes thanking her, but steps to Mother, who hands to her the steaming pot with a small smile. Kuban holds out his cup too. Zarina warmly pours. It is as if they are saying, *If you are empty, I will fill you.* It is times like these that the new feeling in our home does not extend to me.

I close my eyes and see the girl, pouring vodka at the stand. This time, I do not wait patiently in line. I push ahead and explain to her sister that a marriage with me would spare Aigul a life peddling vodka to pushy, alcoholic men. A life with my family would bring her comfort, and she would bring more warmth to us. When I arrived home, after a day spent in study, I too would have a girl to greet me.

Aigul would listen in on the proposal, holding in her eyes that innocence mixed with wisdom. We would agree silently that I could take her.

THAT EVENING WHEN KUBAN, without prudence, presses to his wife in the kitchen—catching her, giggling, against the cupboards—I again hold the picture of Aigul before my eyes. Her quiet face keeps me company that night, while I find sleep in the wake of their lovemaking. In the morning, it is just me and Kuban, for the first time in weeks. He asks, sincerely, "What's new, brother?" He looks at me now with, I think, pity. He thinks that I'm alone. So I tell him, "I have found her, the girl who will marry me."

He lowers the newspaper and says, "Is it true?"

I nod and break into a childish smile. He grabs me and shouts, "Oh, brother, finally we'll all be so happy!" He pulls me into some kind of dance, as if we were together inside the dark of the bar. He has Zarina's sweet and familiar scent, made unfamiliar on him.

"You'll wake the whole house!" I say, pulling from his grip. He sits, his little eyebrows drawn and raised, and starts asking questions, making plans.

"She's already accepted? How long have you known her?"

"Not long. She's new at the vodka stand. But she hasn't—it will not be like with you and Zarina. I'm not her beau. It will be a surprise to her when we come."

"I see," he says, and I cannot read his solemn face. My heart feels a little loose in my chest, unsure it's in the right place. "But you believe she'll make you happy?"

"And I believe I'll do the same."

"The vodka stand," he repeats in wonder, and my heart regains a steady beat.

As I describe to him her beauty, he begins to sketch a map of the market. Mother and Zarina enter the kitchen and hasten to prepare the food, knowing better than to interrupt or ask about the shouting. I'm again too late to avoid Father, and he joins us at the table, giving our whispering a weary glance. But it reminds me of the old days, only better, because Zarina is here, and soon, Aigul will be too.

KUBAN AND I SPEND A FEW DAYS together in my car, tracking the girl's habits. Nazgul never leaves her sister's side: all day they're together at the stand. Their mother appears at midday, a basket of bread and fruit in hand. Before night falls, the sisters close the stand and walk together—careful, it seems, to follow a crowd. Their apartment is not far, in just another tall building of prefabricated concrete. These old Soviet apartments are small, and I'm certain the family must share one room. Once we even get a glimpse of their father, a drooping, unimposing man, as he walks with them one morning. I wonder aloud if Nazgul has been stolen before and escaped. Their caution is not extraordinary, but it is clear.

"I have an idea," says Kuban. "Why not offer Usen or Azamat the sister? Take them both at once. They might even struggle less if kept together."

"That's a good one." I laugh. Usen has very high standards, even in his whores. We tease him it's just a veil for his preference for other men, but he's remarkably immune to our chidings. Azamat can be convinced into almost anything, and the truth is he's so dim-witted that for him to win a decent bride, we really would have to drag her to him. But Kuban does not seem to be kidding.

"Why not?" he says. And I find I cannot say; he sounds so earnest and obliging, almost hurt, that I somehow feel an idea of mine has been dismissed as well.

Though I did not picture them along so soon, I assent. "We'll bring them tonight," I say, "and make the proposal."

We pick up the boys outside their factory. They're disappointed when we tell them it's not to drink, but they perk up at the thought of a double-kidnapping. It has been just a week since I found her, but the season has turned, the air humid, pregnant with summer rain, and Aigul now pours the vodka with swiftness and accuracy. When a red-nosed man grabs for his cup, startling her pretty face, I acutely feel her vulnerability.

"That girl is some chick," says Azamat. "Let me out. I need a vodka."

"That's Bakyt's girl," says Kuban. "What do you think of the other?"

"That dog?" says Azamat. "To steal her would dirty the tradition."

"This is insulting," says Usen. "You tell us the night, we'll get the girl. Even if we have to knock the ugly one unconscious."

"They follow the crowds," I say. "They walk in daylight. It won't be easy."

"Do you want this girl?" says Usen. "Is she the one?" He gives his most impatient look, the one that has time only for unequivocal truths.

"Even Usen is becoming a romantic," I remark, and receive a snicker from Azamat.

"No," he says. "Even you."

"I knew," says Kuban absently. "It didn't take weeks or months. I knew right away."

For a moment the only sound in my car is the radio, forever stuck on a station of Chinese talk, some looping stream of propaganda. Zarina had been in my car once before the night she rode in the trunk. Up front, she sang along to the noise, pretending it was music, and Kuban tried his own competing song. I asked them both, harshly, to shut up. I did not admit I liked to hear her voice, sweet like a mother's.

"That's the only girl for me," I say.

"Tomorrow, brother. We will help you go get her."

MY FAMILY DOESN'T SPEAK of my impending marriage during the meal, but Mother has made an arsenal of bor-sok, urging reserves of the bread onto my plate and observing in her neutral way as I chew. I don't know how I eat; I've no desire for food. Father finally throws out a palm to block my plate and says, "Enough, enough; it's not a dying man's last meal," and Mother kisses my head on her way clearing the table. Father has not asked how I intend to support a wife, and I suspect the smaller part of that is in deference to Mother, to let her see my happiness first secured, and the larger his own lack of confidence in the plan.

Kuban and Zarina linger as I take to my evening reading, and when Mother and Father have gone on to bed, Kuban retrieves from the cupboard an open bottle of vodka. He says, to Zarina, "We haven't even finished our own celebration, already it's time for another."

She giggles and takes her own swig after his. Offering a smile, she holds the bottle to me, and I close my book. "You two drink. I think I'll go upstairs."

"Bakyt, no." Kuban's hand comes to my shoulder. "Stay and talk to us. It's our last night to have you to ourselves."

I hesitate, then take the bottle from his wife, wiping her lips from the mouth with my shirtsleeve.

"I wish we had the cake too," Zarina says. "I can almost taste the sugar on my tongue."

"I wish we could live that whole night again," says Kuban, and they share a look of meaning before she turns away.

"Yes," she says. "I was frightened, but I would do it again, all the same." Her gaze comes to mine, and she leans in close. She smells of cooking grease, and her breath blows across my ear. "Women know," she says, "the compliment of being stolen, even if they fear it. You're a sweet man."

She recounts for us then the excitement she had felt when she saw my car lurked the square. It was a great challenge, she says, to play unsuspecting, to keep from throwing a wink over her shoulder to her love. It seems she speaks only to me; I clasp the bottle to my chest, no longer sharing, trying to recall Aigul's small, steady hands.

"My heart," she says, "it was beating so fast. You were terrible to follow me for so long. Lucky, too, that you snatched me first. You had me dangling like a piece of bait."

In truth, it might have happened, though maybe not like that: some other man could have gotten to her first, before she and my brother met. She could have learned to love that man. I say as much aloud, meaning to show my well wishes and approval, withheld during their courtship. The vodka has hit my heart, speeding my pulse, and the next words come before I realize them. "I would have grabbed you myself. You were too beautiful that night."

Zarina faintly smiles, and I remember Kuban. "Anything for my brother. I believed that you were taking him away, but now I'm glad to have you both."

"There was no real danger," Kuban suddenly says. His short little eyebrows are drawn and raised on his forehead. "No one else could have made it to her first. You won't have to worry about anything like that."

Zarina's eyes are shining as she stares off down the hall that leads to the stairs that lead to the bedrooms. "I felt that way," she says, "that the danger was real. I felt wanted by all men. Every car on the street was alive, watching me, the headlights their glowing eyes. They would do anything, and you would fight. You would fight me. It shames me to admit I liked that."

"You should not be ashamed to admit what you like." I close my mouth, sensing I have gone too far, but my brother only says a line of our mother's, "Shame and danger are close friends," and takes his wife's hand.

THE GLOOM OF THE LIBRARY'S windowless reading room is a shock after the days spent tracking Aigul, hot breeze running through my car, but I settle in at my table, thinking I may not be back for some time. Girls stolen unsuspecting often require convincing, and this may take longer than the course of one night. I will want to make Aigul feel welcome, I will want to show her my love. I will do this by being there for her, as Kuban was for Zarina.

I know Zarina's *you* is Kuban. I know she must have meant fight *for* me. We were all drunk; but last night as I listened to Kuban's panting and Zarina's drawn-out moans coming through the wall, I thought of her passionate kicks against my car trunk. I covered my head with my pillow and dreamed of stealing every girl I saw, no matter if I really wanted her. Bruised and squirming in the sack upon my back, they all wanted out. But to get to me, or escape from me, I didn't know. I was afraid to open it and find out.

From a dusty book I read that in nomadic times the man chased the girl in an arranged race on horseback. She had an early start and a whip to fend him off, but if he could catch and kiss her, her father would consent to the marriage. It was a game, everyone came to watch, and often enough the girl wanted to be caught. I find this old tradition to be beautiful and true, but it's been debased by time—first to the grab and run, *ala kachuu*, on the village street, and now I must fetch my bride in my falling-apart car, with the help of my young brother and two hooligan friends. Aigul will have her sister and her own two feet; I will follow behind, yet I will still be in the lead. But I'd be turning my back on that pull from the past if I tried instead to court and marry in the modern way.

There are other ways to follow tradition. I might pay a bride price to her father, she might load a dowry, had she one, onto a camel's back, we might slaughter a horse for the feast and serve koumiss. But these gestures are so small—the formality and exchange of coin reeking of the whorehouse—and Aigul is as deserving as Zarina of a large one. And what occurs to me now is that she and my brother did it all wrong, their own lust before loyalty to the heart of the act. To be truly kidnapped is to be taken unsuspecting; to be married is to learn to love a new place, captive together in your own country.

I return the book to its shelf, disturbing dust into the stale, dry air. My coughing echoes in the silence. The resources of this room are infinite; there is enough for everyone. I will miss coming here. I don't know that I can ever reclaim my stake, my long, unfettered days. If only Father understood the beauty of this system. His concerns are too practical: need, value, and exchange. Nazgul said, *Our father plans to open one more stand.* Mother said, *Who will take care of you when I'm gone?*

THE MARKET AT EVENING is swarming with people. The crowd parts around a woman and her baskets of red peppers. It seems everyone carries a watermelon: men tuck the fruit under an arm, women cradle them like children. Rugs hang flat and heavy in the humidity. The sun is slipping, but the worst of its heat has been caught in my car. Azamat swipes a palm of sweat from his forehead. Usen nudges the bottle to my shoulder, and I take a long, searing gulp. As the crowd starts to thin, Nazgul emerges, a sack of empty bottles slung over her back. Aigul trails close behind in a light-colored dress, eyes cast to the ground, dark pretty lashes.

"She rides the backseat," I remind the boys, "not the trunk."

"She can sit in my lap," says Azamat.

"We'll take good care of her," says Usen.

"Ignore them, brother."

I am so used to being the driver that I startle when the car begins to move. Kuban has a way of jerking the wheel to change lanes.

"Come on come on come on," says Azamat, singsong. I'm not sure if he's urging the girls along, or the car. "Come on—"

"Will you shut up?" says Usen.

My heart is pounding the way Aigul's would be, if she only knew. She leans to pick a flowering weed come up through a sidewalk crack, and Nazgul, hefting the sack, waves her sister along. At an intersection they cross the street, and we make the same turn. They're following closely behind a young couple with three small children. The husband leads them to an apartment building, and they disappear inside. Ahead of the girls now are just four prattling women, each cradling a watermelon.

"This is it, brother. Won't get better than this."

We're blocks from the market square, and that much closer to their building. I know Kuban's right, but it feels too soon. There was momentum that built stalking Zarina for so long. There was a strange promise in every time she disappeared that she'd return. While Zarina in that white dress against the dark became a ghost, a restless female soul, these girls remain real. They're tired from a day of work, heading home to their parents. The direction of their lives is a real force to them, and I'm about to pull one from that path onto another.

"Maybe, not yet," I say. "Maybe we should wait."

"Are you kidding?" says Usen. "For what?" His voice is loud and angry from the vodka. Azamat laughs, at me or Usen or something out the window.

I watch Kuban's foot as it presses the gas, and I know he's doing it for me. He accelerates until we're nearly at their heels. He stops and says gently, "Go."

Usen and Azamat tumble from the car and yank open my door. My brother lays a hand on my back. "Think of yourself."

Nazgul has turned, and through the windshield we lock eyes. She has taken her sister's hand, and they are running. And so am I.

The girls dart cleanly through the prattling women, but Usen smacks into one of them hard, knocking the watermelon from her hands. It falls to the pavement but doesn't break. The women cluck at us, saying, "Oh, no, you don't. Not again. This has to stop."

Aigul keeps turning to check our gain. We're closing in. Nazgul must sense the futility in running; she wields her sack and gets a good slam to Azamat's side before Usen wrangles it away. It smashes into the street with the chime of shattering glass. The boys push Nazgul to the ground, and she's screaming, "You son of a bitch! You bastard son of a bitch!"

And I know she's speaking to me and not them.

Aigul stands patiently as I approach. "I am Bakyt," I say, and she looks to the ground, those pretty fluttering lashes.

I hesitate, and still she doesn't run, so I seize her arms, so thin and delicate in my fists, and pull her toward me, pressing her tiny breasts to my chest. Her body remains stiff, a separate entity that won't relax into mine. She smells just as much of vodka as I must. The sun is still slipping, and there's a heat to her hair like nothing else on her body. We must look strange embracing, my hand thrust inside her hair, swallowed. *I am married*, I think, *I am married*.

The boys have used the ties and gag for Nazgul, and Azamat straddles her, whispering to her ear, or kissing it. Her eyes are hard stones pointed to the sky.

"Azamat, let's go," says Usen.

"Don't worry," he says, coming to his feet. "We don't want you, you ugly dog."

I place my hands on Aigul's shoulders and steer her, flanked by Usen and Azamat, to my car. As if gagged too, she doesn't call to her sister. I don't worry for Nazgul. Once we've left she'll be untied by the women, who stood watching all this time. As we brush past, they avoid our eyes.

Kuban greets Aigul kindly, but she has no words for him. Usen buckles her in the seat, reaching across her lap, and she flinches.

"Are you all right, brother?"

I rub my wet eyes. Am I all right?

I am married.

AT HOME ZARINA TAKES AIGUL into her arms as though
our purpose were to unite them. Father and Mother sit
calmly with tea at the table and do not look to me. Zarina
pulls a chair for Aigul, and Mother scoots close, saying,
"Do you know why you're here?"

She says that she does, and I'm so proud of her calm,
but then, without a sound, tears start to come one by one,
streaking her round, pretty face. Mother speaks to Aigul
softly, and Zarina says to us, "It's better, I think, if you
leave."

Father gravely nods and stands from the table. He and
Kuban lead the boys outside. Meaning to thank her, or
change her mind, I catch Zarina's hand, hold it between
my palms. Beneath her soft warm skin hides a fluttery
pulse. She turns the pink of watermelon flesh, and we
split apart. The first time we've touched, and it doesn't
feel as I'd hoped. It feels wrong.

I look to Mother, her ever-neutral expression. She has
always been an impartial observer, even in our most reck-
less moments. I think she watches out of curiosity—not
in a wish to interfere or in warning—to see what kind of
men we will become. She wouldn't go to Father with anything we had done, nor would she resist his judgment if
he otherwise found out.

"I mean it, Bakyt," Zarina says. "You can't know what
it's like."

Father can read shame on a face. I offer him mine; I
join him on the stoop. He's staring into the street, where
Kuban and the boys pass the bottle, yelling to passing
cars. The sun has left the sky, but a stain of light remains,

slow to fade. Already, the air has cooled. The pre-moon shows above in white, slowly filling in.

"I like the feel of evening." Father half-turns. "I'm proud of you tonight. You're taking control of your life, for once."

And who had control before? Not you, Father. Not you.

"I imagine you'll want to take the girl——"

"Aigul."

"I imagine you'll want your own place. The house is getting so crowded. I'll pay for it, until you've found your own two feet. There's no need, these days, for everyone to share."

"I would pay for it myself," I say. This remark requires no response. It's a hopeless protest, a sign held up mutely. I weakly add, "If we leave, it will be our own choice."

Mother appears in the doorframe, and Father goes to her, without having once really looked at me. Kuban has his arms around the boys. He is leading them in folk song. I find myself mouthing the chorus: *Every good marriage begins in tears.*

Father calls to the street, "Better take it to the bar. It'll be a long night yet." To me he says, "I'm going to bed. I've got work in the morning."

I wish that for one moment everyone could be still, see that this is my life and it is changing. Mother comes to kiss my head, but she is needed in the kitchen. Kuban and the boys are moving toward my car. Azamat throws himself to Usen's back and is heaved to the ground. Outside the car doors they wait, Kuban on the passenger side.

"Go ahead," I say. "Go on without me."

"Don't be a shit," says Usen. "It's your wedding night."

"Your girl isn't ready to give it up," says Azamat. "Come on. Come on come on."

Kuban jogs over to the stoop, eyebrows drawn in concern. He says, "Brother, she needs time. She doesn't know you yet."

"And how will she if I leave? What will she think of me?"

"She will think you're giving her time."

"I'm not in the mood for those fools," I say, gesturing. "I won't be associated with them any longer."

"They're your friends, Bakyt. They've brought you your bride. They want to celebrate with you."

"What's to celebrate? My bride doesn't want to be here."

"Let Mother and Zarina handle it. It's not your place."

"You just want to rub this in my face."

"How can you say that?"

"Zarina loves you, she goes willingly. Now your bride has to bully mine. And if she consents, you'll be rid of me."

"But I don't want to be rid of you. I want us all to be happy together."

"Yes, it's nice to imagine. It's fun to play pretend. A staged kidnapping, for instance, what fun and games. Almost like the real thing, but no one can get hurt, you might think."

"Listen, it's not easy for anyone. You think I liked to gag her? Or them touching her? You think I like what she said about other men?"

"I think you might, because you know she is still yours."

"She's my wife." Over his face has come that solemn, obstructive cloud. "Don't be like this. It's stupid, there's no point."

He lays a hand on my shoulder, but I brush it off. The follow-through brings my arm into his chest. But Kuban backs away and so do I. Even in horseplay, we've never come to true violence. There's too much respect and loyalty between us.

"Get in the car," I say. "You have my keys."

"All right, I'm going." He holds his arms in surrender.

"Brother fight!" Azamat is yelling. "The best kind!"

"Go get drunk, you assholes."

"We already are!"

"You're the one who needs the booze," says Usen. "You asshole shit."

Doubtless, he's right, and it's not such a bad idea. Under cover of vodka, I can slip into the kitchen. I'll pour a round for the women, no matter if they accept. *Drink*, I'll say, *will put everyone in good cheer*—but their soft voices stop me at the door. I hear Mother: "Bakyt will take care of you; he has a good job. You'll be alone with us all day."

And Aigul: "He's so much older than me. An old man!"

And Zarina: "He's a young man, you could do much worse. He only wants to make you happy. And you'll make him less lonely. If it's love you want, I can say, love isn't so different from this."

I must be thinking the same as Aigul: love and understanding may not be so far apart as to be strangers, but the two might never come much closer than friends.

"Take my husband," says Zarina. "I know him months before we decide to marry. He makes me laugh, spends time with me, and I am glad for someone who knows what he wants. So many men just want to play, and I liked to make them jealous, make girls jealous of us too. But Kuban, he doesn't care about them. He says he has been lonely for me. Then, our wedding night: he pushes me to the ground, throws me in the car—I think, I don't know him. How can I love someone I don't know?"

"Yes," says a tiny voice.

"But I was not wrong about him. He is the good man I thought, and we are closer for it. I love him better now; I know him as you can only know one man. He is my husband."

Aigul is silent, and then: "He can't take me unless I say."

"That's right," says Mother, and she tells another lie, another good thing about me.

IN BED, I CAN'T FIND SLEEP. Any distraction may have helped: the lovemaking, even the sounds of crying. But from my room I hear nothing, and it seems like all silence begins here, with me, then spreads without. I know that in the kitchen the talks continue. Inside that young girl, a war is being waged. One faction of her may be saying, Accept defeat, struggle only makes it worse. While another may be saying, Rebellion is the only honest way. And then there is the part that will always be free.

I don't know her at all. I may never.

Toward dawn I hear my car, the whine of its gears and its settling shudder. Kuban stumbles up the stairs, and Mother's light footsteps follow behind.

"I'm so tired I won't sleep," Mother whispers.

"Take a pull of this."

"Your father."

"Keep the bottle. There's hardly a thing." There's silence as she drinks.

After their footsteps recede, I slip out and take the stairs slow. But what does it matter if I'm heard? I am in my own home, and the girl I have stolen is not in hers.

Scattered throughout the kitchen are plates of pastries, half-empty cups of tea. The jooluk is not in sight. Zarina's head has dropped to the table in sleep, hair cascading over her shoulders and face. Aigul, sitting eyes half-closed, jerks upright when I enter.

"Can't sleep either?" I say, taking a chair.

"I'll kill myself," she says. "I'll do it. I know how to tie my clothes into a rope. My sister showed me."

"Don't do that," I say. "It would be stupid. I didn't think you were a stupid girl, or else I wouldn't have stolen you."

"I'm not."

"Tell me," I say, "don't you hate selling vodka? Don't you want something better?

"Are you something better?"

"I also didn't think you had such a mouth."

Aigul smiles, a real smile, showing teeth. I can't help myself—I touch her cooled hair, tuck it behind her ear, and she flinches. I turn my gaze to the naked window. A gold sun is rising, warming the pale sky. Neither Mother nor Zarina thought to draw the curtain, and all night the girl had held a view of blackness and a reflection of herself.

"I think you're very beautiful," I say. "Do I really seem so terrible to you?"

"It's funny that you ask. Considering the circumstance."

From the back of Zarina's throat, a little noise sounds, catlike, but she doesn't stir. I put a finger to my lips. It seems important she not wake.

"I wonder, what's it like?" Aigul whispers, leaning in. "Acting like such an animal. Just taking what you want."

Her small hands grip the hanging tablecloth, wringing it to rope. With her mouth set, without the glint of her teeth, her expression seems more fierce. Kuban would never have to take this from Zarina. She would never give it to him, and he would never deserve it. Father? We were boys the last time he raised a hand, tears held hostage in his eyes, but he might have hit her, proving her point and still winning. I know he just wants the best for all of us, even if he can't see his best isn't ours. On the table, a teacup in its saucer clinks. The cloth is pulling slowly taut toward a wrinkle where Zarina rests.

"I can't make you do something you don't want." Even as I say this, my hope is at its highest.

But Aigul seems more surprised by my words than if I'd slapped her. Disappointed, maybe, that I didn't. The fierceness leaves her face, and she peers down, setting her small hands open to her lap. "Then please take me home."

She is so young, with a whole life ahead and decisions only she needs to be strong enough to make. I have ruined so much by bringing her here. She will never face me at the vodka stand; Nazgul will spit in my face. And having spent the night inside our home, Aigul will be assumed impure by other men. She may never be wanted for marriage again. I ask, with shame, hoping it doesn't seem one last coercion, if this is something she understands.

"Zarina made me feel I can find the right man." She can't know how that is a swipe to my heart, yet she adds, as if in consolation, "I told my sister I would never do it. Kill myself. I would marry the animal first. You're not that. But my family will be worried. It's almost time for work."

"Yes," I say, "for me too."

I tell her to wash up, and she obeys. I wrap the pastries for her family and wake Zarina, shaking her slim shoulder gently. This time my touch is from a brother to a sister, though I have to will it. She squints at the sunlight that's begun spilling in. Aigul is waiting in the doorway, and in an instant Zarina seems to understand.

"Aigul," she says, "please let me speak alone with Bakyt."

The girl looks to me, and I wave her ahead, throwing her my car keys.

"You don't have to do this," Zarina says. "Give Mother and me one more day."

Her eyes are bleary from dreams, but it seems to me she sees all there is, always has; she is wise and not just the sweet, fun-loving girl I thought. Zarina, I want to say, I wish things had been different. What in our history would have to change to put the two of us on the same path? We came this close, the same country, the same house. From here, we can only part.

But I know this would be stupid, and false. Do I really want my brother's wife? Maybe just a little. She is the first woman I have come to know. Maybe it's just jealousy, or lust. But it's not enough to steal her away. Not enough to marry her. Besides, we're talking about the girl. I said I wanted her, and Zarina played her part—as she did for Kuban, because she cares for us both.

"Zarina," I say. "You're very sweet. I'm glad to have you on my side."

"I'm glad you see it that way. Because I am." Her smile seems to me a little sad, but likely it is relief. Relief that I have given up, on the girl, and she won't have to. She doesn't try again to stop me leaving.

In the car, Aigul is messing with the radio. She can only get the Chinese agitprop to be louder or softer. I don't know why, but it makes me angry to find her there. Maybe I forgot she would be.

"Turn off that shit," I say, pulling into the street.

She rolls down the window and lets her hand ride the air. In the bathroom she had wet and combed her hair, and the winds picks it up, blowing it dry and mussing it again. "I want some noise," she says.

When I ride alone, away from Kuban's easy conversation, away from Zarina's song, away from the ceaseless racket of Azamat and Usen, I listen to the looping message carefully, as if it gives good guidance. I don't know the language, but the foreign sounds have become familiar. Certain phrases I anticipate, shaped by my ears into a string of words in my own tongue. *Run for high ground*—that is one.

I once read that when the Mongols first came, my people cleaved to the mountains.

When the Soviets finally left, not so long ago, I had barely entered puberty. Girls were everywhere, and I thought I wanted one, though I wasn't sure what to do with her. Kuban was just a small boy and still knew girls as friends. We had a black-and-white then, and as a family we watched reaction on the streets of our capital newly renamed. Right in the square, a young woman kissed a young man full on the mouth. Backs to a statue, like it was any other night, workers in uniform drank from a jug of homemade wine. I had little understanding of what this change meant for my country.

"What happens now?" I said.

"Now," Father said, "we're on our own."

THE HUT
\\\\\\\

MY MOTHER THOUGHT THE BEST WAY to teach me to be a woman was to teach me to be alone.

The morning of my thirteenth birthday, I woke from a throbbing inexorable dream in the dark, seized by pain. The crippling waves flooded my middle. I lay doubled over, clutching my pink mouse to my stomach, until light broke between the curtains and the landline rang. My mother picked up right away, as though her hand in sleep had been resting on the receiver. Her murmuring moved down the hall, and like an old-fashioned phone cradle tugged by its cord, my body lifted as one piece from the bed. I didn't want to describe to her what I'd discovered, so I simply stepped from the underpants and brought them balled into the kitchen.

My mother stood by the stove in bright batik with the phone tucked to her ear like a little bird. She cracked eggs into a pan and whisked them with soy milk, Tabasco, pepper. I still wore my nightgown, hair wild from its thrashes against the dream. She taught me always to dress upon leaving bed, to splash water on my face, rinse my mouth, and comb my hair, before meeting another person. She said this drew a line between day and night, kept good spirits from demon corruption. This was just the way she spoke, in symbols and metaphors. All she meant by it was: boundaries were important.

Her murmurs stopped when she saw what I held bunched in my fist. She slipped the receiver from her nest of dreadlocked hair and pressed the mouthpiece to her breast to muffle asking, "Is that what I think it is?"

I nodded, unfolding the white cotton package to reveal the stain, a glistening circle set on the bridge of fabric that stretched between the legs.

Without a whisper, she hung up the phone and put a lid over the runny yellow threaded with red starting to lump unmixed in the pan. "Oh, sweetheart," she said, in her bright, disapproving classroom tone. "How about birthday pancakes instead?" Foot on the pedal, she popped the garbage lid for me to throw in the underpants after the eggs.

I wanted her to acknowledge what was happening, but she only pointed me back down the hall. In the bathroom I unearthed the mini-pillow of a maxi pad from its crinkly plastic wrap, smoothed out the sticky wings, and fastened them in place.

I'd just finished breakfast and settled in before the TV with a dose of liquid Tylenol and a hot water bottle, when my mother came in the room zipping up the brown leather rucksack, stuffed to fill its shape. I knew then I was being sent away, as one of her indigenous subjects would be by his tribe.

In the car, stopped at a light before a strip mall, she said, "I've told you of walkabout. There's not much of an equivalent for girls. Mostly they sit around in huts and houses—if lucky, with handiwork. They'll do the same in marriage."

She drove pinching the wheel high between her fingers as though leading it on by the ear. Her other hand trailed out the window with a cigarette, beads clinking along her wrist as she brought it to her lips.

My mother was an anthropologist by training, one who not only watched but joined in on native rituals—once, she'd suffered a brief psychotic break brought on by hallucinogens taken around a fire—but she gave all that up when she got pregnant, with me, for a renewable contract at community college. She'd never married. If I asked her who my father was, she shrugged.

Merging onto the interstate, she rolled up her window, and the talk radio that'd been on all along brought us news of the world. When she took the exit for the little highway heading north, I guessed where we were going.

The cottage was where we'd spent many summers once Grandpa retired from making cars. After he passed,

Grandma had gone crazy fast, and so my mother and her sisters, who normally only saw each other at Christmas, moved her together to a home. She no longer recognized us as who we were. Sometimes, with a hardened gaze of adversarial respect, she called me Janice, my mother's name, and I felt I'd been given a voyeuristic glimpse of a girl unknown to me, a shadow of a woman undressing in an upstairs window.

The lake was four hours away, the cottage ten minutes more, and I napped in the sun spilling in over the dash. At the general store beside the lot with the climbable statues of Paul Bunyan and Babe the Blue Ox, she stopped for food and supplies. Before she got back in the car, she made a call on her cell and smoked another cigarette. Her expression was at ease, neither conflicted nor concerned, as she exhaled the smoke in steady streams through her nostrils and the hoop that pierced her septum.

We drove along walls of trees, mailboxes signaling civilization within. The leaves were slow to turn that year, and most Up North were evergreens. When they broke, I could see patches of placid lake, unscathed by motorboats. Labor Day had long passed, and I should have started back to school, but the spring before, when I confessed how it had been, my mother decided to keep me home till junior high was through.

By the time we pulled into the drive, the sun had dipped behind the forest line. The woods were shady and cool. We parked in the clearing, and she walked with me along the path to the cottage.

I hadn't been since I was ten, and it was less special

than I'd remembered, just a small green-shuttered house with white vinyl siding. My mother paid someone to clean at the start and end of the season, but inside it still smelled shut up. She showed me the pantry lined with pouches and cans and unpacked the eggs, real milk, and butter. I'd only ever poured myself granola or warmed her bean soup on the stove, but she said she had faith I could figure it all out.

Out back under a tarp was a modest woodpile. "Of course you control the heat with this little dial, but fires can be nice and cozy, especially if you aren't feeling well."

I'd never started a fire in my life. They didn't hold the same primal fascination for me as they did for her. I crossed my arms to my chest as she drew close to hug goodbye. The cramps were back, gripping like a low-slung belt over my abdomen.

"It will only be a week at most. Call before then if it's urgent." My mother made a show of turning on the ringer on her phone and brushed my hair back from my face. It had finally grown back enough from its butchering the fall before that she could. I couldn't believe she was really leaving me, on my thirteenth birthday.

I felt the full weight of loneliness before she could have even reached the car. I pictured the slap of her sandaled feet picking up as freedom neared. She could do what she wanted now, all she'd been denied by my stakeouts with schoolbooks at the kitchen table, from which every murmur in the house could be heard, by my sit-ins before the TV, in protest of her class that went till night, postponing dinner. By my being born and tearing her from the enchantments of the jungle and the bush, ending her no-madic life.

I took two capfuls of the Tylenol and curled on Grandma's creaky couch, pulling the afghan off its back. Apart from an ankle broken by my fall from the balance beam last spring, I'd never felt pain so intense. My insides clenched for the expulsion of the tissue that'd been build-ing up. I started to cry, and the sound of it in the empty house belonged to a stranger. For the first time in my life, even counting all the cruelty of my last year at school, never waking up didn't seem so bad.

But I did wake up. Once late at night to deep silence and shadows shifting on the floor. Again with the sunrise streaming through the open blinds and the songs of birds left behind by autumn exoduses. Each time, I took a swig straight from the bottle and tunneled beneath the blan-ket. When I could sleep no more, my bladder full and my stomach yawning hollow, I rolled slowly from a fetal po-sition to stand.

By Grandma's clock, lunch seemed the most appropri-ate meal to make, but looking at the pantry contents, I re-alized I could eat whatever I felt and no one would have to know. At home, my mother instilled a strict healthy diet, reserving baked goods and sugar for special occasions. I couldn't bring the food she'd packed into the cafeteria at school without whole tables of kids taking up their candy bars and pizza plates to leave, noses pinched against the reek of fermented soybeans and the gas they said I'd pass. Even my locker's smell was said to overcome the drift of tater tots down the hall. I rummaged through the shelf, smacking away a box of pilaf. Behind it sat a pouch of dry fudge brownie mix. It wasn't cake, which I was due, but the steps seemed simple enough.

In the frilly bathroom, I found the flow had been light for all that anguish. Changing the pad, I felt mature and medical, as I had in Health practicing CPR on the doll, while all my classmates laughed and shrieked and refused to put their lips to it, should they find the same sick pleasure in it they claimed I felt. Okay, it was blood, cells that could have made the body and bed of a child, but that was just science, and though my body was undergoing a process disconcerting and gross, I was still me. Suddenly, I understood how my mother could study other humans and write up what they did for fun, as though she hadn't done it with them as their friend.

Back in the living room, I discovered that the cable box was still hooked up and flipped to a trashy made-for-TV on obsession and rape. The brownies came out gooey, and I ate them with a spoon. On the screen, the woman who had been raped was kissing a man who looked like her rapist. He pushed her to the wall, a gentle maneuver wholly unlike the shoves I had received, tossed girl to girl, that one time in the locker room. Uncomfortably, I started to recall my dream, the one from the first night, and felt aware of the band of cotton pressed between my legs. *Go to sleep*, I told myself.

The next morning, the cramps returned with renewed strength. I spent the day on the couch and crumpled over the toilet seat, gripping my ankles. In the bathroom stall at school where I spent lunch, I'd overheard two girls saying you could do it all at once, if you only pushed hard enough. I let out a little wail, and the sound within the tiled walls was familiar. I needed something stronger than children's Tylenol, but it was all I had, so I drank. I remembered that on the day I was born, my mother lost too much blood, and each year at my family party, Grandma had liked to point out how lucky I was that my mother stopped being stubborn and returned in time to first-world medicine. The shoves, the pinches, the pat-downs that pummeled me through the locker room, they left their marks; my body bloomed for weeks beneath my clothes. The only bruise that never turned from yellow-brown to black and blue was the one on my wrist, uncovered by a sweater sleeve, that my mother had daubed distractedly with an herbal remedy while I scowled.

I couldn't believe how much I missed my mother, who, for all the guilty vigilance she'd rendered since the incident, I hated half the time, and who half the time hated me. Ever since she'd decided that I would not go back to school, even after my ankle healed, we'd been too much together. Monday through Friday, I hunched over the lessons she'd made Sunday along with plans for her classes, and she hovered over my shoulder with persistent, condescending hints. At worst, she snapped back, and shut herself in her room. At best, she proposed a break, and we threaded beads stretched on the floor as she told stories. My favorite were of the old woman Baba Yaga, who ate children for supper and lived in a cabin that stood on chicken legs, because these were our own ancestors' tales, but she also told me of beliefs held by people more ancient, who lived attuned, she said, to a morality found in nature. Their literal enactments celebrated human instinct and exposed its transgressions when gone astray. From a feminist standpoint, she said, she often had to disagree with much tradition—the way, for instance, marriage made of a woman first her father's, then her husband's property— but she recognized how rites, rules, and taboos could be like safe hands guiding you down a set of steps.

She saw life that way, that it started high and bright and ended in a cellar. I wasn't sure where in the house that put us, but she assured me we were somewhere in the lamplit middle, together.

I once asked if how I'd been treated that year at school could be considered hazing, initiation into a group, and pointedly she pushed aside the plaid button-down shirts and corduroys of my closet to uncover the crutches propped in the corner. "Nice try, kid," she said.

As darkness fell on the cottage and a wind picked up, I finally got up to close the blinds. I couldn't resist peering between before twisting them shut. Once my eyes adjusted from the TV I could see far into the trees, beech and maple branches swaying over a dense patchwork of pine. With so many familiar comforts, I'd nearly forgotten how far north I was isolated. Most houses by the lake were vacation homes, and no one should be in them now. Even so, I slid the deadbolt, which Grandpa, being of the city, had replaced for the chain.

The mess those girls made of my hair I'd been able to blame on myself, and my mother took the scissors to it with a sigh. But that last time, in Gym, the teacher had seen. Again: the close smell of hairspray and sweat, laughter echoing at my back. Then I stood suspended above it all, on the beam. Gingerly I stepped, splaying my toes—below, a stifled giggle. The teacher had forbidden us to look down, threatening blindfolds. We were to find our footing without sight and ground our confidence in our sense of where the beam lay in space. I skimmed air, but it was there. Slowly I advanced. I was going to make it, I was more than halfway, when I made contact with a sudden object—no, another's flesh and bone—and tripped. The room fell forward, its bottom slipped out and dropping. The girls flew back, all ponytails and shrieks, the teacher already yelling. I had just time to place my feet.

The first one took the brunt of my landing with a crack. The searing shocked me through, in my teeth as much as in my ankle. I passed out.

In the night, a storm brought on the cottage thunderclaps and flashes of light, and in the morning, I found a damp tabby mewing on the porch. Her claws had been scratching at the door, scraping desperate woody streaks through the green paint. She wasn't so thin as to seem starved, but she brushed endlessly against my legs and butted her head to my hands. I poured a saucer of milk and let her in. We cuddled on the couch, her body purring, as I tried to think up good names. At noon I called my mother.

"I certainly didn't mean you had to stay barricaded inside all day like a hermit. Step outside, go for a walk, get some fresh air, for god's sake."

"Okay." I fell silent, and she waited. "What have you been doing, Mom?"

"What have I been doing? What I'm always doing. Teaching, grading, tearing out my hair. I miss you, kid, but I meant it when I said urgent. This isn't much of an exercise if you're calling me for things like how to feed a cat. Tell me you're okay."

I said I was okay. I didn't want to leave the cat all by herself after her traumatic night, but my mother said that was what made cats popular pets for eccentric single women: their resiliency and independent nature, their ability to use a box—I could use woodchips from the pile as her litter.

Outside, the season seemed to have turned overnight, closer now to winter than fall, but my mother hadn't packed a heavy jacket. Rain had taken down the leaves and hammered them over the thicket; most deciduous were now bare. I stomped my feet and twirled in circles, as though to make myself, as my mother might say, known to the universe, but really just to stay warm. Mud-caked and pine-fresh, the woods smelled homey and purified of danger. If I kicked around for it, I'd uncover the path that led to the lake. I wasn't sure I could go all that way alone and didn't want to get lost. But I could follow it for a while.

It felt good to be out; pumping my legs, I felt strong. I found myself humming an aboriginal song my mother sang on Saturdays when she cleaned. I didn't really know the words. I didn't want to. From time to time I heard cars passing on the road, as the path curved along it instead of going deeper into the woods.

Roam far enough into the wilderness of your own back-yard, you were bound to cross into another man's land,

and he wouldn't be too happy. Grandpa said that once. He didn't approve of a lone woman traveling the world to escape, prove a point, or find herself, but my mother said none of that was what she had been doing.

I slowed at the edge of a clearing filled in summer with Queen Anne's lace and spattered now with leaves. A pyramid of beer cans, likely broken by a BB, lay in a frozen tumble over a fallen tree. I recognized the label as Labatts. I wondered who it was responsible for all those empties, if a boy had been here, trying out being a man, or if they'd been a secret stash, so some father could pretend he hadn't had that much.

Farther on, straying just off the path, I came across the patch of weed Grandpa always pointed to from afar as the work of either blacks or hippies. My mother hoofed off here one time, for once forgetting me behind. She liked me always in sight when we were with her parents. I toed the many-pronged leaves, thinking of my wish for something stronger, thinking of my lost best friend Melissa, who the last time I came over smoked cigarette butts from her parents' ashtray while I watched. Drugs and alcohol, my mother said, were known throughout history to bond humans through healthy ritual, but also used to treat and hide symptoms of deep emotional conflict. I may wish to experiment as she had done, but what happens to your body, she said, should happen out of love and a sacred choice.

Drugs, like sex, could cast you into limbo, the duskiness of neither day nor night. Under their influence you could get separated and lost. I didn't want anything to *happen*, to find myself out of my mind, and just a body. I knelt to touch the plant and brushed against a clump of spikes that must have been its flowering. I pinched it hard as I could. Deflowering. In Science we'd studied the pistil and stamen, dissecting them from the petals with our bare hands. A drawing had been passed to me like a note. Opening it, I was reminded of the box beneath my mother's bed. Inside, the veined, rubbery tube fit over a metal bulb that could be turned on to rotate and buzz in a low constant hum I'd never heard, not even in the night. My classmates must have been able to read the recognition in my face. My face burned hot then prickly cold. Mad at my mother all over again, I hurried back to the cabin just as I had run from class.

The cat was glad for my return, slipping through my legs in urgent figure eights. I opened a can of tuna, gave her a dish, and spread the rest between white general-store bread. My hands smelled of outdoors. I washed them and sat to eat at Grandma's Formica dinette, sweeping off every trace of sandwich crumbs when I was done.

Really, what the girls at school, Melissa too, had said of me was true: I couldn't have any fun. The only way to *make* something happen—the kinds of things worth keeping secret, worth sharing, if they could earn me a friend, help me to keep one, or lose one the right way, over a boy—was to hang out after dark in undersurveilled parking lots, where ninth-graders with bristly chins patted the chests beneath their puffy coats, daring each another to "Step the fuck up," and I was too prim, too goody two-shoes to do that. My mother, because she had broken free, was singular and strange, and I had to compensate some-how. But trying not to stand out was not the same as fit-ting in.

No wonder they conspired to reach a hand and trip me from the balance beam, no wonder they burrowed chunks of gum into my hair so deep my mother had to chop it off. No wonder they encircled me and the CPR-practice doll, pushed me down, and held my face, taking pictures of our locked embrace on their phones to spread over the school. No wonder they had called me It, neither girl nor boy, shoving me through the locker room and patting my skinny body down in search of signs for either one.

My mother was right. It was time to learn how to take care of myself. When you're grown-up, she said, you'll be the very same person, but you'll be able to look back to a wealth of accomplishments and hurdles cleared, and the defeats of childhood will seem far away, like they hap-pened to someone else.

I checked myself in the bathroom. The flow had slowed significantly, but I might have another two or three days. I hadn't showered since I'd arrived, so I stripped down and in the stall worked up a soapy lather. I dried my hair smooth and straight like the girls at school, dusted my skin with Grandma's powder.

The last time my mother and I had come together up to the cottage, we found Grandma motionless on the couch. She sat in her robe without her eyebrows drawn, her hair white at the roots and auburn at the ends. My mother knelt at her mother's feet, peeled off the slipper socks, and clipped the hardened yellowed nails, started painting them pearl pink. Even if you think no one else will see you all day long, she lectured me on the ride home, even if you don't like who might come to see you, you should look the way you like to look, every day, for you.

I dressed in the room that usually was mine, where my mother often joined me after Lights Out. Grandma had hung needlepoint on the nautical-wallpapered walls. She kept skeins of acrylic yarn in colored bins in the closet and left a few hangers for me. In the rucksack my mother had packed two of the bras I hadn't yet worn. I slipped one on. It clasped in front with a little pink bow, not what I would have expected her to pick out, but it gave my flat, hidden chest a firm-looking rounded shape under the fresh plaid button-down shirt.

The cat hopped up on the bed and curled head to feet to sleep, and I dragged out a bin of yarn and a pair of knitting needles. No more waking late and TV into the night. I thought I could remember the stitch Grandma had taught me one night as my mother sat in the corner, silently threading beads.

The devil makes work for idle hands, Grandma told Grandpa cheerfully in retirement. He would grunt and pull a lawn chair from the shed and slowly drink what seemed like just one Labatts over the course of the morning, while Grandma put the dough that had risen overnight into the oven and my mother shared the crossword with me, complaining we'd consumed enough carbohydrates yesterday. By the time the bread came out crusty brown, we were slathering on sunscreen, and Grandpa had got out a fishing rod. His eyes were twinkly, and

he pinched Grandma's side as she tried to pack the basket lunch, getting slapped away and called an "old horn-
dog." He looked to my mother for commiseration, play-
fully bumping her hip, but she pulled me briskly along to
gather cover-ups and towels. He seemed hurt, but teased,
"What, I'm being naughty? You going to smack me too?"

The day we found Grandma had lost her mind in the
cottage, she shook my mother off before she'd finished
with her toes. "You wouldn't know what it's like, Janice,"
Grandma had said. "You never let yourself close to anyone. You only lived your life for you. To hell with anyone
who wanted you to have the best."

She turned to me, yanking her bathrobe belt to a knot,
and said, "Janice, you can just go to your room and stay
there. No more playing games out on the streets at night if
you can't behave like a nice Catholic girl."

"They thought I was growing up too fast, too wild,"
my mother said, driving the car. "The way she kept
me fed, it was no surprise I plumped up the way I did.
Though Daddy always called it curves." She kept her eyes
on the road. "So they moved me from the city to the suburbs." This made her laugh. I didn't point out that she had
raised me in the same place, because, just ten years old, I
couldn't see what about that could be so pointless or bad.
When we got back from that last visit, she paced the hall
then shut her bedroom door and made the calls about the
home to her sisters.

I found Grandma's cookbooks in a kitchen cupboard
and flour, unopened yeast, and a mixing bowl in the pantry. On my first try, the dough didn't rise much. On my

second, the loaf came out burned from the oven. On my third, a hot slice with butter made a good before-bed snack. I had started on a scarf that wrapped just round my neck, and I folded it away before turning down the covers and climbing in, the tabby purring at my feet.

The evening of the fifth day, I thought I'd call my mother just to boast of how well I was doing alone. The flow was petering, its proof a faint streak. It would soon be time to leave, and I wasn't even desperate for it. I was baking not just for sustenance or for comfort—though I ate plenty—but to improve my skills, cooling chocolate-chip cookies on the counters, bread and pumpkin pies on open sills. I considered wild animals, but firmly felt the master of the house. As new creations baked, I added rows onto the scarf. The cat watched my activity from the patch of sun atop the icebox.

The phone rang three times before my mother picked it up.

"Yes?" she said in the suspicious tone reserved for dinnertime solicitors.

"It's me, Mom," I said.

I should have known. My mother was still a woman, and when she wasn't telling stories or lecturing, her silence must have held the sound of secrets being kept from me. In the background of her pause trailed a male mumbling, too immediate and everyday to be TV. With a swish she swiftly muffled the mouthpiece. She wasn't alone.

She used to speak of the myth of a traditional sisterhood—this had been the topic of her dissertation, winning her a grant for work in the field—but always said that as her daughter I came first, and everything she did, including coming home to her parents, she did for me. Once she was done being angry that it took a broken bone for me to confess about school, she apologized nearly every day for weeks. She said she understood I'd been ashamed. She said she'd never leave me alone like that again, never let what happened to her happen to me. She'd never told me what that meant, exactly. She said she wanted me sheltered.

"Goddammit," she muttered, ostensibly to the man lurking in the room. I pictured his hand, skin rough from unskilled labor, setting on her silk-enshrouded arm. He would lift the sleeve and blow softly on her hairs, as in a game. The unlikely stepfather—he was the real reason I'd been sent away. My mother was saying, "Sophia? Sophie, are you still there?" I hung up.

I ate half the cookies before the TV, cat cradled in my arm, movie after movie displaying scenes of betrayal and women mourning lost love.

I tried to think of anything my mother had taught me about men or boys, but could recall no specific encouragement or advice, only the broadest statements on structures and implements of power and cultures' concepts of masculinity. Basically (she once crescendoed), you're not much of a man if you've never taken advantage of a girl smaller or more intoxicated than you. In Math there'd been a boy who sat in back etching elaborate engravings with an X-Acto knife onto his desk. The teacher dropped the dry eraser at least once every class, bending so her haunches rounded out and dropped to hit her high heels.

If she called on him, he knew the answer. If she didn't, he spent class making snide remarks under his breath until she did. I was the only one who never laughed, imagining what he imagined he'd do alone to her, despite that she was taller and in charge.

I took off my day clothes before a bare window, and when I turned out the lights, I searched and searched the night's shadows, seeing only the limbs and trunks of trees. Grandpa was the one man of both his city and his country house, and the home he'd bought in the suburbs in between. If, in the night, his wife or daughters heard a noise, he was the one responsible for fending off their fears and bad dreams. My mother said I didn't *need* a father and never really shared her own. Where was she, or he, when in the locker room, hand after hand had roughly groped my chest and passed me on to the next? What did it mean, within her theories, to be an It, and was I now more or less safe? I had trouble falling asleep, but what helped was holding my legs together, squeezing again and again, shifting my hips beneath the sheets.

In the morning, the fresh pad I'd worn overnight was still white as snow, so I stripped it off, rolled it up, and banked it into the wastebasket. Moving without it through the house, I felt naked and free, despite a body bloated if not from fluid or gas then from the cookies of last night. I wanted to celebrate that I had made it through, but I couldn't call my mother, who'd been enjoying my time away.

When I opened the back door to test the air, the cat dashed out, chasing an invisible sprite into the trees. I called her name, "Tab-by, here Kitty-Kitty," until my voice grew hoarse and I gave up. From the shed I dug out Grandpa's fishing rod, bait, and tackle. In the corner was an unplugged mini-fridge of unopened cans. I hesitated, but that they were here made him seem nearby, watching over me. I took one, lifted the tab, and instantly smelled his breath, distinct from the smokiness of my mother's. My first small sip was bitter, and I poured out about half the can in drizzles along the trail.

At the lake, I set his fishing gear on the dock and dangled my feet from the edge, staring out at the rippling peaks. After lunch, before he went out in a skiff, Grandpa stood apart skipping stones with little flicks of his wrist, as though sulking, as though giving us one last chance to forgive his tipsy teasing. The razor-edge caught the surface and bounced, caught and bounced, caught and bounced, sending out concentric waves, then sliced through and was swallowed. I rubbed my thumb along the flat smoothness of a rock, but he had never shown me how and I didn't want to lose it right away. I could see my breath and should have been colder, but another can of Labatts kept me warm. It seemed that, at any moment, ice could strike and spread across the surface, as a flash of light reflected from the sky. I threw out the stone and with a blip it sunk.

When Grandpa died, my mother took charge, advocating for cremation and the spreading of his ashes out over the lake. Her sisters seemed relieved; they just didn't want to have to help. But Grandma's family had invested in a mausoleum, and that's where Grandma wanted him, where she would be. My mother said that now the cycle of the earth could never accept him. No one ever went to see him, and I hadn't asked why: I hadn't been that close to him either. I lowered his gear into one of the canoes tethered to the rocky shore. I wasn't getting in. I'd never figure fishing out. I shoved it off. Either the canoe would fill with rain and snow and finally sink, or it would freeze in the middle, a monument. I watched it slowly sail.

Eventually the sun lowered. I had to pee and I shivered. On the walk back my stomach growled, but I was Eve before Adam, the woods peaceful and still. Not until I reached the cottage, left lit like a confection, did I realize how dark it had become. I set out on the dinette warmed slices of bread and pie and a plate of day-old cookies and devoured it all, leaving the dishes at the table. With cold, tingly hands, I carried more cans in from the shed. Then I came back for some wood.

Over the layer of ash built up in the hearth I stacked the logs into a teepee—I'd seen this on TV. I crumpled up several pages from a paper dated the year Grandma had been taken to the home and sparked one after the other with a match torn from a book from Grandpa's favorite downtown union bar. The flames, consuming fuel, ate hot toward my fingertips, and I kept letting the crumpled ball go before it caught. Finally the fire safely spread. I sat right in front of it, proud, the chemical glow burning my skin. I thought about the marshmallows I'd seen in the pantry but decided that was juvenile. Instead I had more Labatts.

The flames danced, intertwined and apart. I found I could imagine into the fire changing expressions of a face, looking back at me. Now threatening, now inviting, now blank. It was fantasy to envision the voice on the other end of the phone my father returned, and I wouldn't even know what to picture. My mother, with her family, had given me a concrete shape; they were the body that contained me. But there was a wildness running through my veins, the secret of my blood. In the absence of his image, I feared the man I would see. Instead I pictured one for me: the boy from the back of class, hidden by his ballcap brim, pale fur over his lip.

You have nice eyes, he said, peering into them. I drank.

A nice nose. He held a finger before its slope. I finished the can.

Nice teeth. He licked a hot tongue, drawing me close, radiating heat.

It was then that a brightness seemed to jump forth, coming alive. I swiveled over either shoulder; the smoke, wisping in threads, might obscure it. At the edge of my vision, something flashed, a solitary slice of light. It seemed to move as a part of me. I could control it even as it danced and grew. I raised the arm inside its flickering orange cone. I was on fire.

I came sober fast. The flames had caught me only by my sleeve, and I rolled against them on the ground, gasping out of breath. My heart thudded in a way that filled my ears, and when it slowed I felt deafened. Before the smell of singed cotton sent me to my room, I lay a moment in dull surprise that the only danger I'd been in all week had started with the wandering of my mind. I'd always thought that despite Grandma and my mother, I could stay sane.

I woke early in bed, the night a nagging dream. Despite a vague throbbing on my forearm, I didn't remember the fire right away. My body moved heavily, hungover more from the food than the alcohol it had absorbed. With no cramps, no stain, no ritual of a pad to change, I felt I'd lost a companion, an opponent. I felt alone.

At the mirror I washed my face, rinsed my mouth, and combed my hair. I looked different to myself, fuller in the face, and I recognized that I'd somehow become more distinct. My mother knew exactly who my father was, and whether he had treated her well enough or very badly, she saw that capacity in me, in the eyes, say, that were his same devil blue, in the squared-off jaw that followed his shape, in the complexion of my skin, which tanned to island rum while hers burned and blistered in the sun. There may have been others, any number of days of waking in her tent alone, a lover so recently departed the sleeping bag was still warm, so new she hadn't even caught his name; weeks, months, even years may have passed since the last one had gone, her body taken to sleeping as I spied it now, with legs spread, arms tossed, over the empty space. It was even possible—and in revenge for her liaison, the lightness of her week relieved of me, I allowed myself the thought—that she woke once off a trail, wet wound in her hair, pants pushed to her ankles, with no memory of what had occurred. But parting from him, she'd kept me, and I'd never let her forget the circumstances and existence of him.

Some knowledge you inherit, through a mystic kind of ancestral memory. I think that day at the cottage I already carried inside what my mother was really hiding from me.

I held it against her. When she could admit, much later, the ways in which her father harmed her, I realized it was observations of his touch, not of my father's, she pained to see.

I called my mother at home, but when I heard her voice—hopeful, penitent—I couldn't speak. She knew that it was me.

"Sweetie?" she said into the silence. "Is it over? Did the bleeding stop?"

PATER NOSTER
\\\\\\\

OUR MATRIARCH WAS on her deathbed. She was finally giving up. No one thing in particular was killing her, just the cumulative effects of over eighty years of living and abetting life. She was getting what she wanted, which was to die a peaceful death of natural causes in her own room.

By night the news had reached us in our separate corners of far-flung states, and we had each made arrangements to convene on the house. We packed black. Our planes rose over city lights and surmounted mountain peaks, left craggy coastlines behind for the pull of the middle, descending on a piece of patchwork anchored by brick and cement. Home.

Lorna, the last to leave and our firstborn, was the first to set foot inside, politely pushing past the hospice nurse, who warned she was asleep but not that in recent weeks she'd become a slip of skin and bones, hair white as the sheets. Lorna pulled up a chair beside, and that was how Hilde found her, staring off, with her scarf still wrapped and her feet tucked on the seat. She quickly hung their coats and made them tea.

Hope and I caught the same cab, and in it she turned from me, folding her arms and watching crows lift from the lines that stretched above the endlessly repeating silhouettes of roofs at dusk. She had that same smell I used to mistake for warm, salty bread or an evening spent swimming.

When we got to the house, Hope showered, Hilde ordered Chinese, and Lorna lit the wicks that stepped along the candelabra. The pooling wax dripped down with specks of dust. In the room I held her hand, light as a feather, cold. She smiled a wan smile without opening her eyes. At the table, we spoke in whispers of the unseasonably snowless streets, like it could happen all at once, the rattle of her death calling us down the hall.

Last, and close to midnight, Jon arrived without his wife and child, toting like the rest of us the requisite technological attachments to his work. On the porch he set his bags, overflowing from their pockets the chargers and cords, and we poured out the front door, flitting like moths in the light. He was the baby, her favorite, and our only brother. Now we could cry. She could let go.

Surrounded by the five of us, she lifted the lids from her eyes. They weren't jaundiced or bloodshot, just a little tired. Slowly she spoke, lips thin and dry, "I never saw the reason for so many kids." *Until now*, we all pined for her to add. But she had long stopped the practice of lying for our sakes and that was what we'd grown to more than love of her, to respect.

"Can we get you something, Ma?" Lorna asked.

"I think this pillow is too high," Hilde replied.

"Go on," she said, closing her eyes. "I'm not dying tonight. The beds are made, there's extra blankets in the closets."

WE WOULD TAKE OUR OLD ROOMS. Such ownership was still assumed though they now bore little resemblance to what we knew, sterile as a hotel's. Jon's was on the first floor next to hers, while we girls were all upstairs. He would sleep, if he could sleep, with his door open to the hall. The levels of the house had a way of holding sound. What happened upstairs rarely carried down, and vice versa. He joked he should have brought the baby monitor his son had outgrown so we could listen out for her.

"What if you needed it again?" Hilde asked, as though innocent of his wife's thwarted desire for a second child. She'd tricked him into the first, and Jon, sweet Jon, had nearly left her. The "nearly" was embellishment to impress us, we knew. Our matriarch's affection for him hadn't lessened.

"Obviously he'd have brought it back home," Lorna said. "None of us are needing hand-me-downs anytime soon."

Jon smiled his indulgent smile. The only one of us a suburban home owner. Lorna leased an apartment, the extra bedroom for her cats, Hilde a condo, I a loft, and Hope a room in a renovated Victorian, with a wraparound porch and turrets, shared kitchen and bath. For those of us used to the folded shadows of a smaller space, a house—any house, but especially this one—seemed at once too much space and not enough: for our matriarch alone, for her death.

Upstairs Lorna took the smaller, outer room, her elder status giving out a first impression of predominance. Hope, Hilde, and I filed through to the larger, fitted with three twin-sized beds. Hilde next to the bathroom, I next to Hope. The walls served more as suggestions, and Lorna passed through for the toilet, we to go downstairs, fetch a forgotten belonging, a charger, a glass of water, a glance at her. Lying in the dark, we could tell by each other's breathing who was asleep.

"Do I have to put in earplugs?" Hilde asked. "Lynette, do you still snore?"

"I don't know," I said. "What if you miss something?"

"Put them in," said Hope. "We'll wake you up."

"I don't trust we would hear the same things."

"Trust Lorna," I said. She was the one who always heard our father's ghost trapped in the walls, or so she said. To fit he'd have had to lose much more than his body in weight, become a slip of a soul, a repressible presence. No one else ever had a sense of him.

NOT SINCE SOME COLLEGE HOLIDAY had we all spent the night beneath its roof—this house we had all grown inside, just as we had in her, this house whose threshold she first crossed as a bride cradled in the arms of her groom, and through which she had last seen him, our father, also carried, stiffening on a stretcher. From that day, strung across a range of ages eleven to twenty, we watched as she and every trapping of the house, from furniture to decoration, began to change.

Walls were stripped of paper and painted white, the taint of whisky blotted out. The gas stove was exchanged for an electric, a microwave. The velvet-upholstered, high-backed couch and wide-set seats that sagged and creaked went for a slim stiff sofa in stripes and a pair of floral chairs curved to match a body's shape. The shag carpet was torn up for the hardwood, and old photos were replaced by prints of lavender in its fields and street scenes of Paris. Where curtains had blown, blinds rattled and banged. The heavy smell of cigarette smoke disappeared.

At first our own rooms went untouched, only growing more teenaged, due to us. Suddenly she didn't care about the mess left by tacks and tape, the havoc wreaked by our stereos and our shrieks. Instead of taking long walks, she rode a bicycle. She dropped her clubs and took a typing class; forgot to cook, reading books. She told us marriage was a trick and we had better get good jobs. She told us none of us were dying in this town or having kids. The one time Lorna warned her he was still there, she got slapped lightly on the face.

"What do you hear, exactly?" I asked her once. "Pacing? Whistling?" Things that in life he'd rarely done but that an anxious spirit in his prison might do. I must've been sixteen or seventeen, a year or two after his death.

"Begging," she said. "Pleading." This was impossible to believe. He'd sat in his sagging chair, smoking and drinking, in want of being left alone, if in want of anything. "He went against his will. He wasn't ready."

Lorna must've been making a dummy of him, letting him speak for herself. We took with us our clothes and record crates, Hilde to college out of state, then me, then Hope. The rest would go in garbage bags, the concert posters, the strands of beads hung in the doors, the tchotchkes of Buddha and incense sticks. Lorna saw Jon to his high school graduation, and he left with his jug of soldiers, tiny green men melded to their guns, and our father's souvenirs of war: the knife in its leather sheath, the dog tag and medal, the German coins. Lorna held onto her job as a teller and her routine of frozen TV dinners with Ma.

"If you don't leave," she turned finally and told Lorna, "we both will start to rot."

Lorna left, and our matriarch gutted her room, finding our secrets written on the backs of torn-up flaps of wallpaper behind her bed. *Jon's a Republican. Hope's a whore. Lynette fingers other girls. Hilde wishes she was me.* Only the latter wasn't true, or was true in reverse. We never really forgave Lorna, but Ma said she'd already known. Our father made us this way. She'd fixed what she could fix, what was worth fixing; which, out in the wider world, where we'd get worse, wasn't much.

Hope rolled toward me in her bed, then, blinking, back away. She'd left the blinds slit open for the moon. Streetlight fell on her, on me, in bars.

"You smelled like sex," Hilde said. Her voice floated from her chest up to the ceiling rather than across the room. "When you got in. Is it something regular?"

"No," Hope said softly. "Some guy from the plane."

UP EARLY THE NEXT DAY, we fought for the bathroom mirror: Hilde cussing, Hope closing the door on her face, me spitting from the window a mouth of toothpaste. We bothered with brushes and powders not for her or for ourselves but because of each other, the old competition revived. Downstairs, Lorna had dragged in another chair and taken up a post next to Jon beside her bed. They had her sitting up and taking water.

"Are you hungry?" asked Hilde. "Can we get you something to eat?"

The fridge held the haul from the hired woman's last shopping trip. For months she had been telling whoever thought to call that Ma wanted only boxed sangria and chocolate bars. This week she had stopped eating at all. Lorna hadn't changed the order. Over the stove I started scrambling a pan of eggs. I had the heat too high, and they were sticking. Hilde sniffed but said nothing, draping bacon over the contraption As Seen on TV like wet clothes on a line. We'd each been sent one, once, for Christmas. I didn't eat meat.

"Do one soft-boiled," Jon said, pouring juice into the first of five glasses. "For Ma."

She took one bite and spit it up. She took another on her tongue and swallowed back, looking to Lorna for her satisfaction. Hope fled the room with a hand on her mouth. Behind the bathroom door she retched, familiar rhythmic heaves. "One more?" asked Lorna. Gently, Hilde took away the spoon.

Because in the latter decades of her life our matriarch hadn't made her wishes or how she felt about her past a mystery to us, we weren't expectant for last-minute confessions or requests. Yet once we had all set aside our breakfast plates, Hope with me on the floor, Hilde leaning in the door, we found we couldn't leave. Not for a breath of air, not for the dishes. A kind of sacred wash or field of energy flowed from her. I clutched an empty coffee cup for its solid mass, its fleeting heat.

She felt it too, her sway, and it romanced her back into being a mother. For an hour, her slide reversed. She let Lorna stack her pillows, and we listened without leading questions as she spoke. Images summoned themselves, demanding description, culminating in less than stories. Conclusive summaries.

She told us of the slum to which she'd been born. Every shack had since been razed. With neighbors, they'd shared an outhouse, standing barefoot in line on cold nights bright with stars. "There was a smell come up the hole you wouldn't believe. It was the babies."

She passed over our father, who met her at the laundry where she worked, and told of giving birth, from Lorna to Jon, under twilight sleep. "You could have come from anywhere. I don't remember a damn thing."

She narrowed in on Lorna, seeking acknowledgment and not approval. "In eighty-seven years, no sin has brought regrets."

For that hour she was our hearth, our beaming television, with her dying light. Through the blinds behind her propped-up skull, her still-glistening mouth, snow started to fall. From his pocket, Jon's phone came to life, grinding vibrations. He silenced it. She fell asleep.

"YOU DIDN'T EAT MUCH," I said to Hope in the hall. She seemed to me as slight as ever, but her collarbone was not as pronounced, her knees not knobby through the nylons, her hips and butt not without curves. That pale blonde hair, those pale green eyes. The rest of us were dark as Dad and stood with the unflinching bearing of our mother.

"You didn't either," she said, meaning no bacon, only eggs: a crime in this country.

"Are you ever going to forgive me?" I asked, taking her elbow through the arm of her cashmere sweater. Her jaw-line had a new softness making her more difficult to read.

She brushed me off. "Whatever do you mean?"

THAT AFTERNOON THE NURSE RETURNED to explain what to expect and leave us a bottle of pills. She wore street clothes and no makeup or jewelry. Despite the close-cropped hair and the vocation that probably added to her age, she couldn't have been much older than Hilde or Lorna, which gave them license to exchange looks behind her back. She spoke with knowingness and sympathy, but we knew her, our own mother, better. She was strong and never lost without a final fight. Even on her deathbed, she wouldn't be another vessel on the river, pulled along.

"It could be days, it could be months. If she has trouble sleeping, nightmares, hallucinations." She held up and tapped the orange prescription bottle, cascading pills. "But once you start her on them, you can't really stop."

Of all of us, only Lorna believed in the necessity of drugs. Hope slept with strangers, Hilde took home her work, Jon had his family. I was no longer in thrall to my own suffering. The example of our matriarch had taught that it worth learning to live with yourself.

"Would you like help changing her, or with a sponge bath, while I'm here?" The woman held her neck out in a way that'd jangle earrings, had she worn them. I thought a pair would lend to her authority.

"We're fine," Hilde said, and showed her to the door. She and Lorna, so far, had been the only ones to do the wiping down, the diapering.

Jon went to pick up pizza from the family restaurant, the institution, where all of us, at one time or another, had served. Dark syrupy pitchers of Coca-Cola, cheese that pulled in strings, concave circles of pepperoni pooling grease. White sneakers, black aprons, nametags exchanged with coworkers. Nobody could go unrecognized in this town where they knew your uncle from your smile.

"I saw Mrs. D'Agostino," Jon said, exchanging plates warmed in the oven, the way we did only at home, for boxes of pie. "Old biddy still works the front register. She said she was so sorry to hear—" His voice broke, and headfirst into the oven he started to cry.

THAT NIGHT SHE SCREAMED, visited by hallucinations. Jon was up a half hour before an unabating fear drove him to seek female expertise. He'd given his son the bottle, sang lullabies, and slept an hour before heading back to his firm. He'd vanquished monsters from beneath the bed, not once raising his voice, deporting them in fair proceedings from the closet. In our doorway, hoarsely clearing his throat, his silhouette might have been mistaken by bleary eyes for another, impossible male's. *He*, apparently, was who she'd seen: in her own doorway, and then hovering above the bed.

"Your father," she gasped, with darting, dilated eyes that settled, at last, on me. "Your father just had his hands around my throat."

"Ma, that's not possible," Hilde said, though the skin of our matriarch's neck did seem in the mild lamplight flushed, even mottled.

"I'm sorry," I said, smoothing the tangled sheets over her leg. As though detached from her body, its own animal, it flinched. The pills were sitting on the bookcase beside a framed moonlit Seine.

"What was he wearing?" asked Lorna, and thus revealed she had not merely heard this ghost. In my mind's eye he would have on either the short-sleeved dress shirt and tie in which he'd been buried or his buffalo check flannel, the weekend wear in which he'd died.

"A priest. I want a priest." Our matriarch reached out, eyes wild, fingers clawing for what was near. Nearest, now that I had backed off: a nightgowned Lorna, whose own hands were clasped and wringing. "You'll call a priest."

"Of course," said Lorna, with pursed lips that said she was pleased. Our matriarch accepted her hand. Down the hall, a heaving retch. The toilet flushed. Hope had fled or failed to enter the room.

AT THE DINING TABLE, Jon studied dosage instructions on the pills while Hilde found a list of the medication's side effects on the Internet to recite. I'd put a slice of fridge-cold pepperoni on a plate and was picking off the concave circles, piercing my nail into the wax-hard pools of grease.

"How am I going to get a priest?" Lorna said. Despite her earlier uttering of "sin," Ma hadn't been much of a Catholic since marrying a Protestant. Once grass had grown over Dad, she refused prayer at other funerals. She even dispensed with the ritual of preparing a dish for potlucks, though it made her unwelcome at wakes.

"Look one up," Hilde said, offering her wireless device.

"You know what I mean."

The table seemed to straighten up. Jon watched askance as I slipped a pepperoni in my mouth. My stomach lurched

in what I named not-unpleasant surprise. It was harder to
deny a thing once so palpably near and now near again,
wrong or not.

"I'll call Father Molloy," said Hope. The silky sleeve
of her robe slid from her once-bony shoulder as she
shrugged. "I used to steal wine with Toby Cruz, then
sneak into confession. He never told a soul."

THEY SENT A NEW ONE, younger than us all but much
taller, clearly wet behind the ears. Beneath his winter coat,
he wore the collar and a pair of corduroys that stopped
short of his ankles. He leaned in, bent at the knees, to
shake our hands in both of his. His skin was perfectly
dry, as though powdered. Father Molloy, we gathered
from his diplomatic intimations, had been transferred, not
retired. His time had come, at any rate. Jon showed him to
her room, or rather, kept at his heels, briefly transformed
into the puppy that was the youngest son. We heard our
mother ask him to close the door.

The two were alone, murmuring, silent, murmuring
again, almost an hour. We sat in the living room on the
stiff striped sofa and curved floral chairs.

Hilde looked desperately to Hope, who, despite Lorna's
having been assigned the role, had become our official
priest point person. "Can't you—do something? Stop him?"

We were, of course, worried she would confess. And
then, what, there'd be a trial, a witch hunt for accomplices?

At last he called us to come in, stand over her
deathbed, and pray. Wearily, without eyeing each other,

we joined hands, mine to Lorna's, then to Hope's. What began, to my ears, as an incanted babbling issuing too eagerly from the green priest, soon melted a hardness in my throat, then in my chest. Our mother, lids lowered and lightly breathing, seemed at peace, more skeletal and receded into the sheets. When it was done, Hope squeezed my palm. Her face seemed a little green. Lorna was mutely weeping, the sobs gaining a strangled sound and growing in emphasis until Jon took her aside and held her, patting her back.

Hilde led the priest onto the porch, trying to get him to herself. But he reached out to Hope. I let the glass door close, shivering. Beyond the three of them, fresh fallen snow followed the contours of the yards, the low shrubs and curb-parked cars, sparkling. Through the glass, nothing was muffled, all clear as a bell.

"How far along?" he asked. His touch upon Hope's arm, insofar as the man was a proxy of God, was like an impregnation. She flushed a hypernatural red. We stared.

UPSTAIRS, IN THE DARK: "Three months."

The blinds were twisted tightly shut. I could tell by Hilde's breathing she was awake, and angry. I held mine steady.

This was further along than the time she'd called for me. I lived a five-hour bus ride from Hope's creaky Victorian, her hilly college enclave. The foliage was changing, some leaves tinged with green and others fully sunset red and sunrise orange. The city I'd left behind was still sweaty, and here blew a gentle breeze. I didn't know how it was with men, how it could be that in such a community she didn't run out of them or into trouble—more trouble than this. She was a clerk in the science library, a bad one, often absent from the desk and shaking her pale blonde hair out from the bun. In one of the house's only two claw-foot tubs, she lay soaking in a bath. Her floormates, restless in the hall, told me they'd nearly broke down the door.

"I lost it because I'm bad," she said emptily, pinging the filmy surface of the water with her wrinkled fingertip. Everywhere you'd think to shave, she had shaved. What hair was left was more like down.

"No," I said. "I'll show you why." I was exasperated by her helplessness, drained of patience by the ride, but that alone doesn't explain it: I was possessed.

I yanked her from the tub and half-wrapped her in a towel, dragging her past her floormates, scattering from the hall. I locked us in her tiny room, taken up entirely by the antique wardrobe and wrought-iron queen-sized bed. Before the full-length mirror behind the door, I let the towel drop and cuffed her wrists as she tried wrestling away. I traced the jutting of her hip, bumped the ladder of her ribs, once she gave in. I cupped the sharp point of her chin.

"Do you see? This is why. This is what they see, what we all see. You barely care to be alive."

Late into evening, I did not relent, not until she consented to being checked into a clinic. I didn't listen to her loss or give her time to grieve. I didn't get that she'd miss what we'd always said we never wanted, what itself had barely been alive. This was her real secret, one between her and me.

It was like a fourth, unbreathing person in the room now with us and Hilde. I shifted in bed, as though to push it farther from me in the dark.

"Will you get rid of it?" asked Hilde, straining from her natural tone of imperative to one of curiosity. She'd done it once herself, at least.

This was not too far along, but Hope was silent.

"We shouldn't tell her," Hilde said finally. "We shouldn't tell any of them, not now, not here. Are we agreed?"

Even in the darkness I could feel the glow emanating from Hope. The paleness was a front. It was so obvious now. It didn't weigh her down; she'd always thrived on the power of a good secret.

"That priest wasn't supernatural," I said. "You keep throwing up, and soon enough someone else is going to have suspicions."

IN THE MORNING, our matriarch made the request of a soft-boiled egg and ate every bit. Jon, the golden boy, kept to her bedside, the two of them chatting it up, while the rest of us held a hen meeting in the kitchen.

"It helped!" said Lorna. "The priest. She just had to be believed."

But the hospice nurse said this could happen, a sudden turn for the better before a precipitous drop for the worst.

Hilde was ducked in the oven, scrubbing, rubber gloves up to her elbows and soot on her nose. The hired woman had never touched it. "Believed that what?"

She hadn't done it. It had been purely medical, an accident, a mistake. Whatever she'd done, she'd done alone. We all knew what Lorna meant, what our matriarch, mum, had never claimed but Lorna needed to believe. And yet she wasn't ruffled. She leaned over the counter Hilde had just cleaned, cupping her face in her palms like a teenager.

"Don't you think we should ask about the house—who's getting it?"

Hilde sat back on her heels, took the gloves off, and gaped. Hope had an absentminded air and one hand on her stomach. Where there had been a flatness, a concavity, was, for the time first in her life, as on our father, something of a belly, a bump.

"Are you that much a child?" Hilde asked.

Lorna's expression, sulky, defensive, said yes. "Or the china? The crystal vase? Those are sentimental, they're from their wedding."

Next would be the diamond ring our matriarch kept in a jar of flour in the cupboard. If the hired woman hadn't found it and put it elsewhere, one ambitious day baking cookies.

"I'm going out for some air," I said, but no one seemed to notice my voice came from the foyer, or that I zipped up boots, buttoned a coat. They would have heard a slamming door, but, unpossessed, I had no flare for either entrances or exits.

It's not as though I wasn't worried I would miss it. It's not as though I turned the ringer off on my phone. It's that they, as always, were stealing the show.

MUSCLE MEMORY SENT ME OFF toward our old primary school, with my boots breaking the crust of unshoveled walks and displacing tufts of packed-tight powder. An early-morning plow had carved out the street, and the last hour's sugaring failed to refill it. The next house down was where Hilde's high school on-again, off-again had grown up. Lorna had liked him first. Out front, a boy and girl were pushing an enormous snowball. I waved to demonstrate I was no threat and kept going. My fingers turning red with cold and ears already numbing, I kept going. If desperate for a hat and gloves, I'd steal some from a snowman.

At the playground, I knocked snow from a swing and had a seat. Here, beneath the slide, I had fingered other girls. All were consenting, but none had offered to reciprocate. Not until college were they willing, and for much more, up to and including setting up housekeeping. To this day I have said yes, and yes, and yes, then no.

More than once, myself, I had imagined waiting for him to pass out in his chair, then pressing a sagging pillow to his face. But it was more what'd happen after he was gone, what did—where I would next direct my rage—that stopped me.

I didn't have the stomach anymore for the swing. By the time I reached downtown, Main Street was slushing at the corners, trampled by prints, rutted by tires, and yellowed by dogs, but no one was out. Where the doughnut shop had been, sparse and masculine, was a homespun cafe. Ruffled curtains, crocheted napkins, dimpled baristas in kerchiefs. I didn't dare give one a second look when at the counter ordering a basket of scones and a bottomless pot of tea. Huddled by the fire, I turned in to hide my face. Out the window at my back, dusk was collecting in wait of my long walk home.

The living room was lit flickeringly by TV. Jon sat up from the sofa, swaddled in an afghan, his hair mussed. "Are those seriously your mittens?" he said, frowning.

Evidently, I had missed quite a scene: Ma wanted no one to have the house. She wanted it burned, or exorcised. She believed Lorna now about the ghost. When they turned out the lights, her tossing wrung the sheets into ropes. Between shrieks, she bit them in her teeth. In the end they'd given her the first of the pills, and she'd slipped right off to sleep.

EVENINGS, JON STOOD OUT on the porch, his argument or conversation with his wife coming out in muted puffs. Hilde had taken over the dining room with her laptop, spread of papers, and conference calls. Each night, Lorna scolded her to clear the table so I could set it. Back and forth into the kitchen, for the stack of china plates, the fistfuls of silver, Lorna offering critiques of how Hope sliced the vegetables and tied the legs of the chicken, fretting intermittently over her cats, which she had left to the care of a "close friend." We knew we were supposed to misinterpret him or her as a lover.

I, too, kept tabs on work by checking emails, deleting most. I, too, ate the chicken, concentrating on the crackly skin. Of all the meats, I had missed this one the least.

In and out of awareness, our mother shrank. No curtain call, but it was again her show. "I feel like, what's growing inside me, it's taking from her," Hope confided, Hilde asleep.

I thought of how, meaning to unseat Lorna from what we all saw as a high horse, Hilde had lured from her the boy next door, offering to go between and in reality repenning her love letters in her own hand. The typed letters Lorna believed written by him in return subtly undermined her sense of superiority through backhanded compliments and growing descriptions of time spent with her sister, extending from her deliveries. Hilde confessed before any finale, for in the process she'd fallen truly. But about that fact, repentant, she was forever after changing her mind.

Hope had never shown herself to be enamored. I swore to her we kept her secret because it wasn't ours to tell, not because its revealing would give anyone pain.

In this way a week passed, and then another week.

"I CAN'T STAY HERE FOREVER," Hilde said. "I'll lose my job."

"I've already lost mine," Hope said softly.

Jon, a junior partner, was on paid leave. He was sheep-

ish as he admitted, "Amy's finally agreed to bring Nicholas. They're on the red-eye tomorrow night."

"You're flying out your *family*?" said Hilde. "Your son
is *three*. That age can't sit still, much less stay quiet. How
will she ever find the peace to leave with a kid tearing up
her house?"

"Lynette?" Lorna said sharply, calling everyone's attention to me. "Can you stay, or do you have somebody
waiting?"

"A little longer," I said. "I can stay."

THE BOY WAS UNLEASHED on the house in a torrent of
giggles, skidding rugs from their grips, tipping over picture frames. We each had met him only once, flying out
in Hilde-arranged pairs (I with Lorna, she with Hope) the
year Amy was nursing. Like Jon before he'd gone dark,
his defining features were towheadedness and sticky
hands. But while Jon from the start had been serious and
studied, preferring to be by himself—even when I, lonely
square in the middle, offered to ride bikes into the farm-
land or play catch—his toddler son did not hold back, and
seemingly was not often asked to.

"Nicky, please give hugs to your aunts," Amy said,
in lieu of hugging us herself. She stood back, behind the
roller suitcase, ludicrously, in sunglasses. The day was
gray, the city she'd left filled with fog.

The boy plowed right for Hope's stomach, then, no-
ticing her top jean button undone, grabbed for it and
laughed at her. Paling, Hope excused herself for the bath-

room, the boy still clinging, cackling. Jon distracted him with some good old-fashioned roughhousing. He gave the boy a noogie, the boy fought back, both collapsing to the floor as we looked on from above.

"How's she doing?" asked Amy.

No one answered. She'd given our brother a son with the spirit of our father, a bully of sorts. Our mother she'd never liked. When Jon hefted him to his shoulders and to her room, explaining in a hush, "Nicky, this is your Grandma. Ma, this is Nicholas," the boy, crinkling his nose, said, "Why does she smell like that?" Luckily, she was under the influence of the drug. They had a better encounter later, after Lorna and Hilde changed her and administered her sponge bath, before her bedtime dose. He curled up at her feet—"Careful, Nick, she's very sick"—while Jon read from a picture book he'd dug up from the basement. On her lips was the faintest of smiles.

That night I was awoken in the room I shared with Hilde and Hope by a sound. A sound that, if I'd not dreamed it, could only have come from between the walls, because noises never carried from downstairs. A muffled pleading, or a moan. Hilde and Hope breathed the breath of sleep. In the next room, Lorna had thrown off the covers, drooling spittle on her pillow. I pressed my ear up to the plaster. Unwittingly, Ma had painted him in. I waited until I understood—not *never*, I remembered, but *rarely*; we were above the living room—and waited some more before creeping downstairs. I wanted that woman to know I'd heard her with my baby brother. Maybe her baby, on a cot in Jon's room, had heard too. Maybe our dying matriarch.

Amy had slept the red-eye off through dinner. Now she was in the fridge, rustling for leftovers. She turned swiftly, clutching for her heart inside her breast. "You startled me!" Of course Jon told her everything, from the ghost down to the directive to be childless: she was his wife. I reconciled myself to orienting her in the kitchen, then stayed to keep her company. She surprised me by wanting to watch over her.

"The truth is, she frightened me," Amy whispered both as though she were and weren't already gone. "I still don't understand what she had against me."

Was that what life on this earth was for—to understand the meaning of everything? What smell came up the outhouse hole: fetuses miscarried, aborted? Had Ma or Hilde bowed to perform mouth-to-mouth? Long ago, I'd made a home of what was inside and let all else lie where it was, in varying degrees of obscurity. No matter if I'd revolted him or showed now some of his qualities—to withdraw, to turn aggressive—he no more ruined us than Ma could save us. Unburdened, I'd been happier, no longer haunted by images of easy escape: spilling pills, bathtubs overflowing, waves of gas heat roiling from open ovens. I'd saved myself from myself. And I believed a woman dying or so alive she was growing a life was entitled to her omissions. Or a defense.

Because then Amy whispered, "I'm worried about your sister," and nearly smiled. "I know, right, which one?

You're the only one besides Hilde and Jon who has it together. Hope. She's looking, well, fleshier. But you know she was throwing up in the bathroom."

She surprised me again, by blurting before us all at the breakfast table, "Jon, why didn't you mention it wasn't only us newly expecting?"

THE HOUSE WAS SHOWING ITS SEAMS, full to bursting. Hope, brushing me off, broke out on an empty stomach for a long walk. Hilde took conference calls on the porch, coming in to refill her coffee. Lorna rummaged through the basement for other sentimental items to claim, and I kept to the corners, gathering laundry and rubbish. In the garage Jon got our matriarch's car running, and Amy drove it twenty miles to the mall, bringing back discounted designer perfume for herself and a snowsuit for Nicholas. All day, the boy was up and down the stairs, distributing toys, stopping only for an hour's nap. Lorna made tea as we swarmed late afternoon and darkness fell, making mirrors of the windows.

"Look," said Lorna. "We need to all sit down and listen to Dad. You can't comprehend how his soul suffers— he was back at it last night. I've thought of nothing else. We need to put him at peace."

Bereft of the benefit of sunglasses, Amy lowered her eyes. Her husband met them. Gave her the nod. The nod that meant she should go someplace else. She scooped up Nicholas and stuffed him, all wriggles and shrieks, into the suit, leaving behind her acrid cloud of perfume.

"What exactly are you saying?" asked Hilde.

"A séance," I said. In the basement, doing laundry, I'd seen the Ouija. One load, at the bottom of a stack of games; the next, the whole thing toppled and Ouija missing. In her search for valuables, Lorna must have felt inspired to slip it out.

Hilde looked agape from me to Lorna. "Right now. With her—still in the house."

Hope's hand went to her belly, a gesture she no longer had reason to hide was protective. Just as she had when, earlier, Amy outted herself as well as Hope, Lorna did nothing to acknowledge it.

"Yes," Lorna said. It was clear nothing less would satisfy her than a door opened to the unknown. I was willing to give this ghost, because it was hers, one last chance. Maybe, even if it was real, it couldn't hurt or possess us. Maybe even in the face of losing our matriarch, all five of us were capable of keeping it together.

Lorna dimmed the fixture and over the table spread a dark red cloth from Christmas. Tealights lined the sills, blinds lowered. I lifted a slat. The night was purple, bright with snow. The girl and boy from next door were being pulled past in a sled by a father figure, Amy and Nicholas nowhere in sight. Lorna moved aside the burning candelabra to set the board out in the middle. It smelled of our childhood, a mix of box-new plastic and stale cigarette smoke. We'd never played this one, all five of us, at once.

We set our fingers, two each, on the pointed plastic piece—the planchette. Felt feet for easy gliding and a window through which to see. It was difficult to hold them there without wavering, which would itself exert a force. Jon lifted a finger to scratch his nose. Lorna, of course, would play the medium.

"Is there a presence in the house?" she asked. Nothing happened.

"Dad? We know you're there. We want to hear you out."

"Is she with you?" Lorna whispered. "Are you together?"

I felt a subtle pressure on the planchette. The hospice nurse had said our mother might take the chance to slip away when left alone, but I'd like to give Lorna credit. Maybe all she meant was she was close. On the cusp of life and death, where in the shadows a ghost could take shape and make use, again, of his hands. The planchette lurched and started gliding over the board.

"Oh!" I let out. This reproduced the jolt I'd felt at the sound in the middle of the night, the suspension of disbelief that had me with an ear against the wall. I glanced to Jon and Hope. It was useless. Hilde was pushing it.

YES.

"Will you let her speak?"

The planchette darted from and back to YES. We let it.

Lorna waited, as though his ghost were handing over a mic toward which the newly credentialed ghost of our mother was shuffling.

"Ma," she said, "you know we've never asked you to explain anything that happened that day, but it might help Dad if you—"

Already, the planchette was swiftly swerving over the letters, pausing to spell:

F-A-V-O-R-

Too late, I saw Hilde would go too far again.

Hope and I hadn't been there, a summer afternoon too ripe to stay inside. In his sagging chair, drink sweating by his side, he'd yelled at Jon for dumping out the jug of soldiers to use the shag carpet as his jungle. Too old to be playing with dolls. Too old to be acting like a girl. Ma banished Jon to the backyard and before the fight began closed the living room door. Hilde heard Ma call for her as she was lacing up her sandals to see her beau the next house down. What kind of scene she came upon, whether he was or wasn't already on the floor, was never clarified by the two. Upstairs, Lorna tossed aside her magazine only at the sound of sirens homing in.

-I-T-E.

"Favorite," said Lorna slowly.

H-I-L-

"Hilde: I knew it. You always said you didn't have— but I knew. That's why—"

Nearly imperceptibly I shook my head. Lorna paused, took her fingers off the planchette, and ripped the board out from beneath, hurling it and hitting the base of the candelabra. The flames stayed upright, yearning for the ceiling, as it tipped. Jon caught it, openmouthed. The board thwacked against the wall, making a mark on the white. Hilde couldn't hide her smile. She, Lorna, hadn't always been this way. Once, she had been our unflappable eldest, always ironing for Ma and getting A's, even setting her hair in curlers for dates. Who could say what made one member of a family and not the next able to right herself. No wonder Ma was tired: even in bearing witness, there was almost no escaping getting caught in the middle.

Lorna stood from the table. "You need to grow up, all of you. In fact, Hilde and Jon, you're in charge of dinner. Hope and Lynette, you two are changing her before bed." Adding, as though we might argue and keep shirking the duty: "It's your turn."

Amid the puffed-out smoke Jon put away the board, while Hilde, licking her thumb, wiped at the wall. Hope and I ventured down the hall.

"Lorna's right," Hope whispered at my back. "Jon's one thing, and anyway, he has Amy, but how am I ever going to be a—?"

I stopped her. From the threshold, the room seemed to hold a new stillness, the stench of shit. Slowly I approached the bed and held a hand out to her mouth. Breath blew my skin. I kissed her papery cheek. Hope, bumping her belly, drew down the sheets, and at the sink I filled the plastic tub with soapy water. Together we eased the sleeves from the arms of our mother.

ACKNOWLEDGMENTS

So many thanks to everyone at A Strange Object. To my editor, Jill Meyers, and her codirector, Callie Collins, who found the book in what I sent them, and whose smart, careful edits helped make it the best it could be. Thanks to Jin Auh for her persistence and her belief in these stories, and to Jessica Friedman, and Alyson Sinclair.

Thanks to the editors and journals who first published these stories: Evelyn Somers, Speer Morgan, and really everyone, at the *Missouri Review*; Salman Rushdie and Heidi Pitlor; Bill Henderson at the Pushcart Press; *Narrative Magazine*; Laura Cogan and Oscar Villalon at *ZYZZYVA*; Kara Levy at *Joyland*; and Justin Taylor and

Minna Proctor at the *Literary Review*. Thanks also to the editors and journals who gave homes to stories not in this book, but who nonetheless were a great support to my work: Dave Daley at *Five Chapters*; Sharon Dilworth at Autumn House Press; *Prairie Schooner*; and Andrew Malan Milward at *Mississippi Review*. Special thanks to Kara and Andrew for their friendship in SF.

For time, support, and community, I am indebted to the Iowa Writers' Workshop (shout-out to Connie, Jan, and Deb: thank you for all you do); Joseph and Ursil Callen; the Provost's Office at the University of Iowa; the Michener-Copernicus Society; the MacDowell Colony; the Martha Heasley Cox Center for Steinbeck Studies at San José State University; and the beautiful Playa residency program in Summer Lake, Oregon.

So grateful for all my teachers—heartfelt thanks go especially to Sam Chang, Kevin Brockmeier, Chris Offutt, Gary Wilson, Peter Ho Davies, and Laura Kopchick, who first gave me the faith to follow this path.

Huge thanks to the collection of readers and friends who, during the ten years these stories span, provided thoughtful feedback, cheerleading, and companionship in writing/reading/dancing/drinking, especially: Erin Brooks Worley, Chris Leslie-Hynan, Akemi Johnson, Julia Green, Matt Griffin, Jennifer DuBois, Els Andersen, Valeri Kiesig, Marion Bright, Monica Bergers, Amy Belk, Julia Glassman, Dave and Kelli Fleming, Kristin Kearns, Cooper Cruz, Matthew Flaming, Josh Shalek, Dahlia Grossman-Heinze, Carrie Toth, Michelle Matchulat, Julia Sobol, and Maria Rousseva. I'm lucky to have had, for over half my life, the friendship of one of the best, most generous people I know, Christina De Giulio: thank you, Tina!

With love and gratitude, thanks to my family, especially Calvin, Alma, and Eli Eib; my dear brother, Eric; my sister, Emily, for also being my bestie; and my parents, Michael and Susan, who have never given less than their full support.

ABOUT THE AUTHOR

Katie Chase's short fiction has appeared in the *Missouri Review*, *Five Chapters*, the *Literary Review*, *Narrative*, *Prairie Schooner*, *ZYZZYVA*, *Mississippi Review*, and the *Best American Short Stories* and Pushcart Prize anthologies. A graduate of the Iowa Writers' Workshop, she was the recipient of a Teaching-Writing Fellowship, a Provost's Postgraduate Writing Fellowship, and a Michener-Copernicus Award. She has also been a fellow of the MacDowell Colony and the Center for Steinbeck Studies at San José State University. Born and raised outside Detroit, Michigan, she lives currently in Portland, Oregon.

ABOUT A STRANGE OBJECT

Founded in 2012, A Strange Object is a women-run, fiction-focused press in Austin, Texas. The press champions debuts, daring writing, and good design across all platforms. Its titles are distributed by Small Press Distribution.